THE PRIVATE
LIFE OF SPIES

By Alexander McCall Smith

THE PRIVATE LIFE OF SPIES

LIFE OF SPIES

Alexander McCall Smith

abacus
books

ABACUS

First published in Great Britain in 2023 by Abacus

1 3 5 7 9 10 8 6 4 2

Copyright © Alexander McCall Smith 2023

The moral right of the author has been asserted.

A CIP catalogue record for this book
is available from the British Library.

Hardback ISBN: 9781408718353

Trade paperback ISBN: 9781408718360

Typeset in ITC Galliard by M Rules
Printed and bound in Great Britain by Clays Ltd, Elcograf S.p.A.

Papers used by Abacus are from well-managed forests
and other responsible sources.

MIX
Paper from
responsible sources
FSC® C104740

Abacus
An imprint of
Little, Brown Book Group
Carmelite House
50 Victoria Embankment
London EC4Y 0DZ

An Hachette UK Company
www.hachette.co.uk

www.littlebrown.co.uk

The Private Life of Spies

Stories from the world of spies

Nuns and Spies
(England, 1943)

Syphax and Omar
(Algiers, 1924)

Ferry Timetable
(Scotland, 1984)

Donald and Yevgeni
(Shanghai, Moscow, Washington, 1934–1947)

Filioque
(Rome, 2022)

Author's note

These stories are part fiction and part non-fiction. In *Nuns and Spies*, one of the common legends of World War II – that German spies were dropped into England dressed as nuns – is explored. For further discussion of this widespread belief see James Hayward, *Myths and Legends of the Second World War*. *Donald and Yevgeni* is based on the life of several historical characters, including Archie Clark Kerr, a British ambassador, and Donald Maclean, a British spy. There is a very informative biography of Clark Kerr: Donald Gillies, *Radical Diplomat*. This biography addresses the question of the unlikely Russian valet, Yevgeni Yost. For further details of the career of Donald Maclean, reference may be made to Roland Phillip's excellent *A Spy Called Orphan*. Finally, on the Vatican Secret Service, see the exhaustive treatment of the topic in *The Entity* by Eric Frattini. There is an immense literature on the *filioque* controversy. The history of this remarkable issue is discussed in A. Edward Siecienski's scholarly *The Filioque: History of a Doctrinal Controversy* (Oxford Studies in Historical Theology).

Nuns and Spies

Conradin Muller was an unusual spy. He was recruited in Hamburg in June 1943, much against his will, and sent on his first, and only, mission in late September that year. He failed to send a single report back to Germany, and when the war came to an end in May 1945, he fell to his knees and wept with relief.

'I never wanted any part of this,' he said to his friend, Sister Cecilia. 'This whole awful, disastrous mess. Never.'

She knew what he meant, and she believed him. 'There, there,' she said, patting his wrist, as she often did when things became too much for him. 'There, there, dear Conradin. All over now. The Lord works in mysterious ways – few can doubt that – but He usually achieves the results He wants. Of that, there can be no doubt whatsoever.'

'I have much to thank the Lord for,' he said to Sister Cecilia. 'For this place. For you and the others. For everything that happened to me. I am constantly grateful.'

And he was. His gratitude, in fact, knew no bounds, and he reminded himself each morning of his great good fortune. He had been a spy in wartime, and had it not been for the kindness of Cecilia and all the other sisters he would have met the grim fate that such spies meet. He owed them his life. He owed them everything, in fact, and one day, he hoped, he might be able to repay them. They were kind English people, and he would not hear a word against the English. Not one word.

Until that fateful day in 1943, Conradin had lived a blameless, if somewhat dull life. He was the only son of Gustav Muller, the owner of a small printing business, and his wife, Monika, a piano teacher and an invalid. Gustav was an alcoholic, and unreliable; Monika could walk, but could do so only with difficulty; she relied on Conradin to do the shopping and the housework. When not helping at home, Conradin, who was naturally gifted when it came to foreign languages, had a part-time job teaching English to science students at the university. He also taught occasional classes in Spanish and French, although English was his main subject. He had studied for three years at King's College, London, before the war, and before returning to Germany had taught for two years at a boys' boarding school in Devon, a place of bizarre traditions and minimum academic standards that went bankrupt when Conradin was on the staff. These five years in England meant that he felt perfectly confident in the language, a fact that unfortunately caught the attention of a local Abwehr colonel, whose brother-in-law was a professor of physics at the same university at which Conradin taught.

On the outbreak of the war, of which the Muller family thoroughly disapproved, Conradin was thirty-eight years old. Men of that age were being taken for military service, and Conradin was interviewed by the local recruiting office. The interview, however, was conducted by a retired army officer whose wife was distantly related to Conradin's mother. This relative had explained to her husband that Conradin was the most dutiful of sons and that if he were to be taken by the army, Gustav would be unable to look after Monika. Gustav's own health was shaky – his drinking had eventually taken its toll – and he, like his wife, relied on Conradin's help. The officer himself was sceptical, but he dared not contradict his wife, and Conradin, to his considerable relief, was duly exempted from enlistment.

This exemption was to prove short-lived: when the colonel discovered that Conradin spoke perfect, idiomatic English, he summoned him to his office and informed him that he was happy to report that his offer to work for German Intelligence had been accepted.

'But there must be some misunderstanding, Colonel,' protested Conradin. 'I have not offered to do anything.'

The colonel fixed him with a steely gaze. 'It would be very unwise to contradict my recollection of events,' he said. 'I take it that you understand me?'

Conradin swallowed hard. He had understood only too well. 'What do you want me to do?'

'You are to be trained as a field agent,' said the colonel. 'You will undertake a three-month course, during which you will be shown how to behave like an Englishman.' The colonel laughed. 'You have to be able to drink tea in a special way if you are to avoid detection in England. In a very effeminate way. Like this.' The colonel lifted a cup with his little finger extended, in a mockery of affectation. 'See?'

Conradin nodded dumbly. This was the end. He would be captured and that would be the end of him. He had no future now – none.

'And you will be thoroughly trained in the operation of radio,' continued the colonel. 'Have you ever operated a short-wave radio?'

Conradin shook his head.

'It is most important that operators should understand how these things work,' said the colonel. 'Not only are there issues of radio wave propagation, there are matters connected with antennae. The correct length is vital for a functioning antenna, you know. There is mathematics involved in that.'

Conradin swallowed again. Was it best to be blindfolded when you faced a firing squad? Or could you simply close your eyes?

'So,' said the colonel. 'That's settled, then. The orderly has prepared the papers.'

He clicked his fingers and a uniformed orderly appeared. 'Sign here,' he said. 'And then here. And here.'

Conradin noticed the orderly's fingernails. They had been bitten back to the quick. He shuddered.

'You are now enrolled in the Abwehr,' the orderly said in a low voice. 'Congratulations.' His accent, Conradin noticed, was Bavarian. There was a faint whiff of beer. They were like that down there, he thought. They liked their beer-halls. Brutes.

Although he was far from being a volunteer, Conradin found some parts of the course stimulating. There were lessons in the geography of Britain, in history – German agents were capable of listing all English monarchs, in order, since Richard III (a 'very fine king' said the instructor) – and in the right way of addressing a duke, an earl, or a baronet. They were also given rudimentary training in Morris dancing and in the various types of English beer. At times, the attention to detail in their instruction was impressive, as when the prospective agents were obliged to sit through an hour-long lecture on the correct way of entering a post office, greeting the postmistress, and purchasing a stamp.

'Do not compliment her on her dress,' said the lecturer. 'Do not address her as *gnädige Frau*, or anything of that sort. Do not talk about anything except the weather. Have you got that?'

There were nods of assent, although many of the recruits were secretly puzzled. How much could anyone say about the weather? Did the English really have nothing else to talk about?

But their lecturer had more to say on the subject. 'And when it comes to talking about the weather, always say that it is fine, even if it isn't. The difference between English and German is that while German is a rational language, in which what is said is what is meant, English is the opposite. In English, if something is large, you say it is small; if a problem is a major one, it is described as being a "little difficulty". And so on. There are many examples – too many to enumerate. Also, remember that the English do not comment on bad conditions, except when it is raining very heavily. Then you must say, "Nice weather for ducks." Do not say anything else. That is very important.'

The instructor thought of something. 'Everything I have been saying applies only to the English. Do not forget that there are also Scotsmen. They are different. If something is bad, then they will say that it is very bad. If it is good, they will usually say nothing, just in case it *becomes* bad. That is also very important, but you need not worry too much about that, as we are not going to drop you in Scotland – unless there is a navigational error.'

This was a joke, and there was laughter.

The instructor grinned briefly, and then continued, 'If the French are mentioned in conversation – let's say you're in a pub and somebody mentions them – then you must roll your eyes and say, "*Mon Dieu!*" That will be quite sufficient.

'If Germans are spoken of, then you must be very careful.

Just say, "So much for Jerry," and leave it at that. If British forces are mentioned, then say, "Good for our boys."'

The instructor surveyed them. 'Is that crystal clear?' he asked.

'*Jawohl*,' they replied in unison.

The instructor sighed. 'You must be careful not to say that,' he warned. 'The English are not stupid. You should say "jolly good" or "right-oh". Understood?'

The instructor looked at them. They were doing well, but there were certain habits that had to be drummed into them time and time again.

'Let me repeat,' he said. 'If you want to sound like a local, you must use certain words that are very important. *Jolly* is one of them. You can add this to anything – and that is just what they do. So if you are asked how you are, you must reply, "I am jolly fine." If you are asked what the time is, you should say, "It is jolly nearly twelve o'clock," or whatever. If something unfortunate occurs, then you should say, "This is a jolly bad show." You cannot use the word too much.'

'Jolly right-oh,' they said.

'Jolly good,' said the instructor.

Conradin was sceptical about this use of the word *jolly*, but he had not been in England for some years and new usages were emerging all the time. It would be best to be receptive to the insights of these instructors, who presumably knew what they were doing.

*

During the war, as in any time of confusion, rumours about German spies abounded in Britain. Officialdom discouraged these, but it was too much to ask that people would not pass on stories that, even if implausible, were not beyond the bounds of possibility. In particular, tales of the disguises affected by German agents were eagerly listened to, embroidered, and then passed on. To some extent, this was the fault of the authorities themselves in encouraging distrust. If people were warned to question the identity of others, then it was not surprising that they might question whether the policeman directing traffic was really a policeman, or whether he was a German agent in police uniform. The Germans, they were told, would stop at nothing in their attempt to infiltrate: the rules of the game, it seemed, had been suspended for the duration.

Historians of wartime myths often cite one particular example of a widespread false belief of the time – that German spies were being parachuted into Britain dressed as nuns. This story was widely circulated, and believed, although it was never backed by any concrete evidence. Like most such legends, the source of the belief is untraceable, although the Dutch Foreign Minister of the time, E. N. van Kleffens, must have helped the rumour on its way when he announced in the early stages of the war that German paratroopers dressed as nuns had been dropped in the Netherlands.

That had not taken place. And yet, with the recent discovery of Conradin Muller's diary in a second-hand book shop in Cambridge, we now have a reliable first-hand account of just such a case. On his first mission in September, 1943, this frightened and unhappy German agent was dropped by a Luftwaffe aircraft over a Suffolk field. He was dressed as a nun, and he carried with him a pouch of maps, a small short-wave radio, a battery, and a Roman Catholic missal. As the drone of the aircraft that had brought him across the North Sea faded away, Conradin looked up past the canopy of his billowing white parachute. He could make out the stars in the night sky – innocent, neutral witnesses of the foolishness of men. It was a strange moment for him. He wanted to cry. He wanted to raise to the heavens a roar of frustration and denial. What had he done to deserve this? He had not asked to be here. History had caught him up in its skirts. And, to top it all, he had to endure the absurdity of this fancy-dress, this nun's habit, complete with elaborate wimple, so ill-suited to the business of falling through the sky towards the unwelcoming earth below. They had told him that it was the best possible disguise; that nobody would suspect a nun; that even the most officious policeman would think twice before challenging a nun and asking her to produce papers. 'Nuns are above suspicion,' they said. 'That is why you are safest if you dress as one. This is confirmed by all sources.'

Conradin disagreed. 'Why don't they dress us up as pantomime horses?' he whispered to the man sitting next to him at their final briefing. 'Nobody ever asks a horse for his papers.'

'It is unpatriotic to joke about these things,' his colleague reproached him. 'Remember, we Germans do not have a sense of humour.'

Preparations for departure went ahead. His nun's habit, when it was delivered, was found to be several sizes too large, but was adjusted by a local seamstress. She carried out the final fitting in her atelier, observed by her young son, who watched wide-eyed as Conradin slipped the habit over his normal civilian clothing.

'*Mutti*,' said the young boy, 'can I be a nun when I grow up?'

'If the Lord calls you,' muttered the seamstress through the pins she was holding between her lips. She winked at Conradin. 'Children,' she said.

'This was not my idea,' muttered Conradin.

Two days later, after a bumpy and frightening flight, with the pilot flying at wave-top height to avoid radar detection, Conradin was bundled out of the aircraft into a cold and rushing darkness. As he dropped down, he thought of his mother. She loved him. Just about every soldier had a mother somewhere, who loved him and who would be hoping for the war to end. Down below, though, in the unlit countryside, were people who did not love him at all, but who wished him dead. He had done nothing to them, but they would happily kill him if they had the chance – nun's outfit or no nun's outfit. How could people hate those whom they had never met? Only too easily, it seemed.

He landed heavily, winding himself badly. As he lay on the

ground, his parachute collapsed over him like a white silk tent, Conradin struggled to reflate his lungs. He thought he must have broken something, and was wondering whether it might be a leg. If so, he would have little chance, even of giving himself up, as he would be unable to move very far and would have to wait until ignominious discovery occurred the following morning. And that, he thought, would be the end of that. There would be a summary trial – if he was lucky – and then the imposition and exaction of the ultimate penalty. The fact that he was dressed as a nun would only make matters worse. The English would not approve – he had no doubt of that. It would be different if he were to change, but he would have no chance of finding a German uniform which he might don. Even civilian clothes would be hard enough to get hold of.

He sat up before gingerly rising to his feet. There was no pain, no sudden collapse of his legs once he put his weight on them. He was uninjured, it seemed, and could walk. The discovery cheered him: it could have been far worse.

He looked about him. He had landed in an open field, which was fortunate, as there were woods nearby and he might easily have floated down into those. There were no lights to be seen anywhere – he had been told that the drop area was four miles from the nearest village and that all he was likely to find would be farmhouses and barns. None of these, of course, were lit at three in the morning, which was the time at which he arrived in England.

11

He bundled up his parachute. Strapped to his radio bag was a small field shovel, and he now used this at the edge of the field to dig a hole in which to bury the parachute. This took almost two hours, as the ground was hard, and full of roots. Eventually, though, he was able to finish the task and to cover the disturbed area with leaves. Then he thrust the spade into a ditch, where it was concealed by mud and water, and started down a small lane that he hoped would lead to the village. He had been told that there were two buses a day that would take him to Ely, from where he could catch a train to Cambridge, where a contact would meet him.

It was summer, and by the time he reached the outskirts of the village, the sun had floated up over the horizon. It was a fine morning, and had he not been dressed as a nun, in enemy territory, he might even have enjoyed the walk along the quiet lane. An inquisitive cow watched him from a field; sheep looked up from their grazing; a bird sang to him from a hedgerow. He wanted to cry. He would readily have changed places with any of these creatures, to be free of this world of conflict and danger that human beings created for themselves.

He had been assured that he would be dropped in exactly the right place and that the very best navigators were chosen for these flights. That was not the case. The navigator allocated to his flight was facing disciplinary proceedings. He was drinking excessively and had received several warnings. His calculations were out by miles, and the village outside which Conradin had been dropped was not the intended one. And it happened that this village was home to a convent of Anglican nuns, the Little Sisters of Charity. These nuns, who followed the Rule of St Francis, ran a large pig farm, a substantial vegetable garden, and a home for those who, in the language of the time, were known as 'fallen women'. The fallen women were taken in by the nuns, looked after during their confinement, and then sent back to their families with the baby, if they wished, or after the baby had been put up for adoption, should the mothers opt for that. Unlike many such homes at the time, they did not exert any pressure on the mothers to surrender the baby. Nor did they seek to lecture the women or make them feel guilty. 'You are all loved – no matter how bad you have been,' was a motto worked on needlepoint kneelers in the chapel.

It was outside this convent that Conradin found himself, turning a corner in the lane, just as a line of nuns emerged from the gate, crossed the road, and began to make their way down towards the pig farm. He stopped in his tracks. To his front was the line of nuns; to his left was a millpond. Above him was a clear, empty sky. It was blue, and free. He looked up. God existed. He must do, or something like this could never have happened. He took his radio bag off his back. He held it for a moment, as if weighing it, and then dropped it into the millpond without making a splash. It floated for a moment, and then sank, disappearing in the murky green water. A duck on the other side of the pond flapped its wings.

The line of nuns was now some distance away, and Conradin had to run in order to catch up with them. But he soon reached them and, as he did, one of the nuns turned and smiled at him.

'I was almost late myself,' she said to Conradin. 'Sister Angela gave me an awful rocket about it the other day.'

Conradin nodded sympathetically. 'I overslept,' he muttered, keeping his voice as high-pitched as possible.

'Easily done,' said the nun. She looked at him curiously. 'You're new, aren't you?'

'Jolly new,' said Conradin. 'Just arrived.'

They walked on. There were six of them, Conradin noticed, all wearing a habit that he was pleased to see was very similar, if not identical, to his own. They were of different ages, he saw – some looking young enough to be novices, while others were in their fifties or sixties. But they all looked very well-fed, he noticed; indeed all of them looked as if they might have benefited from a diet.

'What is your name, Sister?' asked his new companion as they approached the gate to the pig farm.

Conradin hesitated. 'My name?' he asked.

'Yes, your name.'

'Sister Conradin,' he stuttered. As he gave his answer, he realised that here was a glaring defect in his masters' preparations. They had given him identity papers under the name he would assume in Cambridge, but they had said nothing about his identity as a nun. If that was their level of incompetence, then it was no wonder that they lost so many agents.

'I'm Sister Cecilia,' said the nun. 'I'm named after Saint Cecilia, although I'm definitely not musical. My singing is hopeless. I try, but I just can't hold a note.'

'We all have our talents,' said Conradin. 'I'm sure the Lord has sent you other gifts.'

They were approaching the pig sheds. 'Dreadfully smelly places,' said Sister Cecilia. 'It's not the pigs' fault, of course, but they are a bit smelly.'

'Jolly smelly,' agreed Conradin. 'But they are all God's creatures.'

'Don't overdo it,' said Sister Cecilia. 'Some are, maybe, others – I'm not so sure. There's a very ill-tempered sow. She's called Arabella, and you have to watch her. She'll give you a nip if she gets the chance – a serious bite, in fact. Don't let her get near you. Use your slap board to fend her off.' She paused. 'I'm looking forward to eating her, actually. Mother says that we can slaughter her next month and make bacon. It won't come a day too early as far as I'm concerned.'

'I love bacon,' said Conradin.

'And sausages,' said Sister Cecilia. 'Mother has a recipe that was given to her by the Bishop of Ely. He loves a good sausage, they say.'

They were now at the pig sheds and a senior nun was allocating tasks. Sister Cecilia was instructed to clean the feeders littered about the field and then unblock a ditch that ran alongside one of the sheds.

'I'll help you,' Conradin said quickly before he could be singled out by the senior nun.

'You're very kind,' said Sister Cecilia, offering him a peppermint. 'These are very strong, these mints. They're not on the ration, actually. I exchange them for rashers of bacon down in the village.'

'Needs must,' said Conradin.

They set to work.

'You're very strong,' observed Sister Cecilia halfway through the morning. 'I bet you're as strong as any man.'

Conradin bit his lip. I should have been more careful, he thought. 'I come from a strong family,' he said. 'My mother was a strong lady in a circus. You know the sort of thing? She tore up telephone directories. Lifted motorcycles, and so on.'

'That's amazing,' said Sister Cecilia. 'You're lucky. Some of the sisters find the farm work just too much for them. Mother will be very pleased to have you if you can do all these hard tasks. She often says it would be so good to have a few men round the place – but all the men are off in the army or are unfit for anything very much. So, it's just us and the girls.'

'The girls?' asked Conradin.

Sister Cecilia mopped at her brow with a large white handkerchief. 'The fallen women,' she said. 'Has nobody told you?'

Conradin shook his head.

'We run a home for fallen women,' Sister Cecilia said. 'They come here when they find out they're going to have a baby and their families kick them out. People are so cruel. But we look after them and help them to get back up on their feet. We usually have about five or six girls at any one time. We give them light duties in the vegetable garden or they do sewing under Sister Agnes. We have a contract to make pyjamas for the air force. We can't produce all that many – twenty pairs a week, most of the time, but it's our contribution – one of them – to the war effort.'

Sister Cecilia looked up at the sky. They had almost finished clearing the ditch and it was time, she said, to go back for lunch. The other sisters would come back a bit later.

'Have you met Mother?' Sister Cecilia asked as they walked back towards the main convent building.

Conradin shook his head.

'You'll like her,' said Sister Cecilia. 'She's strict, but she's really kind at heart. Some consider her to be a bit of a schemer, but then she wouldn't have got where she's got if she was unable to hatch the occasional plot.'

'I look forward to meeting her,' said Conradin. He was unsure what to do, and had decided he would simply let events flow over him. He had abandoned his mission at the moment that he dropped his radio in the millpond. There was no going back now. He would simply see what happened. If they shot him, they shot him – so be it. For the moment, he would continue to be a nun, which, on balance, was far better, he decided, than being a spy.

Seated at her walnut desk, under a painting of Richeldis de Faverches, the English noblewoman to whom the Virgin had chosen to appear in Walsingham, Mother sighed.

'They keep doing this,' she said, a detectable note of irritation in her voice. 'Mother House keeps sending us sisters without giving us proper warning. Then, when you complain, they say that they did write to us but the letter must have been destroyed by enemy action. That excuse will work once or twice, but after a while it wears a bit thin.'

The Mother Superior looked over her half-moon glasses at Conradin, seated on a hard-backed chair in front of her desk. 'I take it you were in Salisbury?'

Conradin nodded. He did not want to lie; he had had enough of that. There were so many lies back home, and now he had no heart for them. But he could hardly start telling the truth now, at this late stage, seated here in this convent, in a nun's habit. 'Yes. I was there. Then they sent me here.'

Mother shook her head. 'They really are the limit, Sister Bernadette and the people in her office. But, not to worry – the important thing is that you're here. I gather that Sister Cecilia has been showing you the ropes. She said you were very useful down at the pig farm.'

'I enjoyed working with her,' said Conradin.

'That's very satisfactory,' said Mother. 'Some of the sisters don't like working with pigs.'

There was a silence. Conradin noticed that Mother's eyes were on his shoes. 'Those are good, stout shoes,' she said. 'Very useful.'

He swallowed, and reflected on the fact that he was bound to be exposed. It was a miracle that he had not been seen through straight away; it was inevitable.

'I wish I could get a substantial pair of shoes myself,' said Mother. 'Everything on offer these days – even if you have the coupons – seems to be made of very thin leather. Wartime economy, I suppose.' She looked at the shoes again. 'You take quite a large size, Sister,' she said.

'I always have,' said Conradin quickly. 'At least as an adult.' He paused. 'When I was young, I took a smaller size.'

Mother looked thoughtful. 'That's the way of things, I suppose,' she said.

She rose from her desk. 'Well, Sister Conradin, we are so looking forward to having you among us. Sister Cecilia will show you your room – we don't call them cells any more, although some of the older sisters still use that term. I shall see you, no doubt, at dinner in the refectory. We eat very early here.'

He rose too, and inclined his head to Mother in a gesture of obeisance She smiled back at him. 'Blessings, my dear Sister Conradin,' she said. 'And I am so pleased that you have dropped in.'

Dropped in ... The words hung in the air, as if suspended between them. Did Mother know? Was this her way of saying that she knew that he had arrived by parachute, and, if she did, was she now on her way to make a furtive call to the local police? In the chapel tower, a bell was being tolled. Would the next thing he heard be the siren of a police car racing to the convent to arrest him?

Sister Cecilia was waiting for him outside. She drew Conradin aside and whispered into his ear, 'Mother likes you. She told me as she came out. She said she feels you have been sent to us by the Lord himself – to help with the pig farm. She is very pleased.'

He smiled weakly. He had been thinking of something that he would have to discuss with Sister Cecilia and that could not be put off.

'May I ask you, Sister – what are the bathroom arrangements?'

Sister Cecilia did not seem surprised by the question. 'We have bathrooms on each floor. There are more than enough of them.'

He waited a moment, and then asked, 'And are they nice and ... private?'

Once again, Sister Cecilia did not think the question inappropriate. 'Yes, very private. Our order has always stressed modesty. You need have no fears on that score, Sister Conradin. We have never approved of communal washing facilities.'

He felt immensely relieved. Now all he would need to do was to lay his hands on a razor. If the worst came to the worst, he might be able to find a knife in the kitchen that could be sharpened sufficiently to allow him to shave. He would have to do that soon, he thought – no later than tomorrow afternoon. The occasional nun may have a voice as deep as his, but there were very few nuns, he imagined, who had to worry about five-o'clock shadow.

He was exhausted that first night, and sleep came quickly. As he lay in the darkness, in his narrow bed, he felt only relief that he had survived the day. The dread that he had experienced during the flight from Germany, the terror of the parachute drop, the fear of exposure that had attended every moment at the pig farm – all of these seemed to melt away. He was alive, and nobody seemed intent on changing that. He had fallen amongst people whose approach to the world about them was not one of confrontation and anger – as it was back in Germany at present – but of acceptance and love. It was so different, and even he, an intruder, an impostor, felt embraced by that feeling.

Before he had retired, he had participated in the later offices of the day – Vespers and Compline – and had found comfort in the gentle, almost whispered liturgy. Tiredness had caught up with him by Compline, and he found himself drifting off during the reading of one of the psalms, only to be kept awake by a friendly nudge from Sister Cecilia. Then there had been the confession of sins, and as he uttered the words, he realised that he was truly sorry for the wrongs he had done – not that his sins were numerous. He had never sought to harm anybody; he had never wanted to be a spy; he had never accepted the venom of his times; he had done his best to keep away from that poison. But he was nonetheless engaged in a gross deceit, perpetrated every moment that he wore his nun's habit. He was not entitled to that. He was not entitled to the friendship and charity of these women amongst whom he found himself. But what were his alternatives? Were there any at all, other than the firing squad or the noose or whatever fate awaited a captured spy in wartime? His instructors back in Hamburg had said little about that; they had not spelled out the consequences of discovery. He found himself wondering what God, if he existed, would want him to do. God would understand limited options; God would appreciate that not all of us can be brave. God, he knew, would see through his disguise, because God, of all people, could tell the difference between a real nun and a fake one. You can't fool God, he thought . . . and with that in mind, he drifted off into sleep, to dream of pigs who spoke English to him, and a parachute that disinterred itself and floated slowly up into the sky, and of some of those other things, snatches of memory and association, that make up the landscape of dreams.

Sister Cecilia had provided him with fresh clothing. She complained about the lack of attention to these matters by the order's headquarters in Salisbury. 'They should have given you a suitcase with fresh linen,' she said. 'They always forget to give people the things they need. Fortunately, we have plenty here, but it really isn't our job to give new arrivals the things they should have been issued with by what's her name . . . Sister . . . Sister . . .'

She looked to him for help, and he thought quickly. 'Oh, I know the one you mean. Her.'

'Her, yes, her. Sister . . .'

'Oh, I keep forgetting her name. She's so . . .'

Now Sister Cecilia came to the rescue. 'So bossy. Not that I should be uncharitable, but sometimes . . .'

'Yes. Bossy. She's jolly bossy.'

Sister Cecilia nodded. 'You know something? I don't think she can count. No, I'm not making it up. I've seen her using her fingers to add things up. And what's the use, I always say, of having a sister in charge of stores and supplies who can't count for toffee?'

Conradin agreed wholeheartedly. 'She's useless,' he said.

'Well, it doesn't matter,' said Sister Cecilia, pointing to the neat pile of clothing she had delivered to Conradin's room. 'Once you've put those things away, we can go and feed the pigs. There are slop buckets outside the kitchens. It's dirty work, and I can't stand it, but we have to carry those down to the farm. It takes hours, and the pigs are so greedy, pushing and shoving to get their snouts in the trough. They really are disgusting.'

'I don't mind doing that,' said Conradin. He glanced at Sister Cecilia and saw her face light up. Now he insisted. 'You really must let me. I love doing that sort of thing.'

'Would you mind?' asked Sister Cecilia. 'It would free me up to go and have a cup of tea with the girls – the fallen women, you know.'

'Of course.'

'Personally, I don't like to call them that, but that's just me. Mother uses the term and so do the government people who come round here to check up on them. Even the girls themselves use it. It's such a shame.'

'It seems unkind,' agreed Conradin. 'Lapsed, perhaps? Lapsed women?'

'Like lapsed RCs?' Sister Cecilia shook her head. 'I don't think that's any better, really. And it's so unfair. The men who cause the problem in the first place aren't called fallen anything, are they? They get away with it. Do they have to go off to a monastery for nine months? They do not. They just carry on – tra-la-la – getting girls into trouble as if nothing had happened.'

Conradin shook his head. 'Men are beasts,' he said.

'Not all of them,' said Sister Cecilia. 'Some, not all.'

'Of course.'

Sister Cecilia thought of something. 'When you go to collect the slop buckets, be careful not to take the ones with red handles. Those are scraps for the girls' refectory. Don't take those down to the farm.'

Conradin frowned. 'You mean that the fall—the girls get slops too?'

'Scraps,' said Sister Cecilia. 'Not slops. There is a difference. Mother doesn't hold with waste. Things like crusts of toast and bacon rind and so on – those go to the girls. It varies their diet, you see. They are all on the ration. And that can be a bit measly, you know. One egg a week and so on, although they get a bit extra because they're expecting. Still, it's not all that exciting and so we give them the scraps from our table too.'

Conradin asked whether the sisters were also on the ration.

'Oh no,' said Sister Cecilia. 'We have our books, same as everyone else, but we have bags of extra supplies. Mother feels that the rules don't apply to nuns. She's a bit of an historian and she says that goes way back to Plantagenet times.'

Conradin had noticed that dinner the previous evening had been a large meal. There had been lamb chops, piles of mashed potato, beans and homemade mint sauce. There had been a starter of smoked trout and a dessert of rhubarb and ice cream. And there had been second helpings all round, with some nuns, including Mother, having three. Breakfast had been slightly less substantial, but had nonetheless involved copious quantities of scrambled egg, rashers of thick bacon, and fried mushrooms.

'We produce it ourselves,' explained Sister Cecilia. 'So why shouldn't we eat it ourselves?'

Conradin shrugged. 'I don't see any reason why not.'

Sister Cecilia made a dismissive gesture. 'The Ministry of Food sends inspectors from time to time. They snoop around farms to see that you aren't taking any stuff you're not meant to. But those people are no match for Mother. She runs rings round them.'

'How does she do that?' asked Conradin.

Sister Cecilia tapped the end of her nose with a forefinger. 'Best not to ask. What they call the Rule of Silence in Cistercian circles. Know what I mean?'

Conradin did, and asked no further questions.

Over the next few days, Conradin settled into a new routine. He found that the ordered nature of convent life – the regular meals, eaten while one of the nuns read aloud from a life of the saints or a book of devotions, the hours of work at the pig farm, the domestic duties of scrubbing and polishing – all of these lent themselves to a sense of stability and calm that was just what he needed. The war seemed a long way away, the only reminders of conflict being RAF activity at the airfield some twenty miles away. Conradin had been trained in the identification of aircraft as part of his education in espionage, and he found himself gazing up at the sky and automatically counting the bombers as they headed off towards the North Sea. Apart from this, it might have been peacetime for all the impact that the war had on the sheltered life of the nuns and their young women. Conradin relished that sense of detachment. He detested the war and all that it meant, and here he could allow himself to pretend it was not actually happening. Of course, there were moments when he suffered pangs of guilt: terrible things were happening in Germany and elsewhere, and he was doing nothing to stop them, and yet, when he gave the matter further thought, he realised that he *had* done something after all. He had effectively deserted, and that was an act of opposition by any standards. He expected no credit, but he did entertain the idea, half-seriously, that there should be medals for deserters. Surely they deserved them even more, perhaps, than those who simply obeyed.

He had very quickly made himself indispensable at the pig farm. Not only did he cheerfully take on dirtier tasks, such as the clearing out of the sties, he had also assumed various maintenance duties that the nuns had ignored in recent years. None of the nuns, he discovered, was prepared to climb a ladder; he did so willingly, tucking the skirts of his habit into the black tights with which Sister Cecilia had issued him. The roof of one of the barns was in a bad way, and Conradin soon worked out how to replace or rehang the slates that had worked free of their nails. Poking about in the dustier corners of a barn, he found supplies of paint, and he used this on the wooden sides of the agricultural machinery store. He excavated ditches long clogged up with weeds; he repaired fences tested and breached by generations of pigs; he cleared away all the clutter and detritus that inevitably accumulates in any farmyard, a task that in most cases is talked about at great length but rarely done.

He found himself getting on well with the pigs. 'These are intelligent creatures,' he said to Sister Cecilia. 'You can see them thinking, can't you?'

'They seem to like you,' she said.

'And I like them. Pigs are just themselves. They don't try to be anything else.'

'That can't be easy,' said Sister Cecilia, looking directly at him. 'It can't be easy to be something that you're not.'

'They don't try,' Conradin remarked.

She looked thoughtful. 'Do you think they have souls?'

He was not sure. 'They might do. But how would one tell?'

Sister Cecilia thought that you could see a soul if you looked in a creature's eyes. 'I've always thought dogs have souls,' she said. 'You look in their eyes and you see it. You see the longing, the love – the whatever. There's something there, I think. Pigs? I'm not so sure. Perhaps.'

'Of course, if they have souls, then should we eat them?'

Sister Cecilia considered this for a moment. Then she said, 'I love bacon.'

Conradin did not take the matter further, and he noticed, anyway, that Sister Cecilia had fixed him with an intense, slightly unsettling gaze.

'Some animals can see through us, you know,' she said. 'Dogs certainly can, and I think pigs might be able to do so too. Not all pigs, perhaps, but some.'

He said nothing. He tried to meet her gaze, but he found it difficult.

'So, for example,' Sister Cecilia continued, 'a dog can tell whether somebody's lying.'

He pretended disbelief. 'Surely not,' he said.

'Oh yes,' she said, her gaze still on him. 'A dog can tell. They look into your eyes and I think they must see something that we might not be able to see.'

He shrugged. 'Who knows?'

There was a short silence. Then Sister Cecilia said, 'I think they may be able to sense fear. I think that might be it. Frightened people always give themselves away. It's something to do with the way their hands shake slightly – ever so slightly. Much of the time you wouldn't see it, but then you look, and you see that their hands are shaking.'

He made a supreme effort to control himself. He wanted to shake, but he resisted. He tried to think of something else – something innocent. He thought of the psalm that had been read the previous night at Vespers. He had been struck by the beauty of the words. It sounded so far less beautiful in German. But everything did, he reflected. He would stop speaking German when all this was over. He would deliberately forget his German, if you could do that with a language. He would speak English and perhaps Spanish, which was another language he had learned and loved.

He hardly dared look to see if she was staring at his hands. She was, and he immediately put them behind his back. Her gaze came back to his face.

'You must tell me about your childhood one day,' she said. 'I'd love to hear a bit about it.'

He laughed – a contrived, falsetto laugh. 'Oh, there's nothing much to say about that. Nothing, really.'

Then she said, 'Where did you get your accent? It isn't English, is it?'

He was prepared for this. 'Iceland,' he said. 'I was brought up in Reykjavik. We spoke Icelandic, which is like very old Danish.'

'Well, I never,' said Sister Cecilia. 'That explains that.' She paused. 'What does it sound like? Could you say something in Icelandic for me?'

He laughed. 'Oh, I wouldn't want to confuse you. It's a very tricky language.'

'But just say something. Anything. Say, "My name is Conradin."'

He was cornered. "All right,' he said. He cleared his throat. *'Mi naam Conradin iss.'*

Sister Cecilia clapped her hands together. 'But I understood that. It sounds very like English, doesn't it?'

'Some of it,' he said. 'All these languages are more similar than you'd imagine.'

'So what's pig in Icelandic?'

He thought quickly. Then, 'No, there's no word for pig in Icelandic. Sorry.'

'No word for pig!' Sister Cecilia exclaimed. 'There must be.'

He immediately regretted his answer, but it was too late.

He would have to persist. 'There are no pigs in Iceland,' he said. 'Pigs never got that far.'

She frowned. 'Didn't people take them with them?'

He shook his head. 'They tried. Many centuries ago, they took some pigs from Denmark to Iceland, but the pigs did not do well.'

'What happened?'

'They froze. Or that's what we learned in school.'

It took her a few moments to digest this. Then she said, 'It's so sad. But tell me, what do Icelandic people do when they see a picture of a pig? What do they say if they don't have a word for it?'

'They use the Danish word.'

'Which is?'

Again, he had to think quickly. 'In Danish pig is *poeg*. It's very like the English word.'

'And bacon?' she said.

'The same,' said Conradin quickly. '*Bakon.*'

'This country used to get most of its bacon from Denmark,' said Sister Cecilia. 'The war put an end to that.'

'The war,' sighed Conradin.

Sister Cecilia looked at him as if undecided about something. 'It's so sad, isn't it?' she said.

He lowered his head. 'I am ashamed,' he muttered.

She frowned. 'Why? Why should you be ashamed?'

The remark had slipped out. But he recovered by saying, 'Ashamed at not doing more for the war effort.'

'But you're doing your bit,' said Sister Cecilia. 'You're working on the land. That's war work.'

'Perhaps,' said Conradin. 'But you know how it is. You never feel that what you're doing is quite enough.'

Because the fallen women took their meals in their own refectory, and because Conradin had not been allocated any duties in the vegetable garden, where they worked for several hours each day, he had only glimpsed them from time to time. When he took the pails of scraps over to their refectory he left them in the small porch behind the kitchen, and did not even see the cook who would later come out to collect them. In his second week in the convent, though, he found himself delivering scraps at the precise time that the cook, a somewhat discouraged-looking woman in her late forties, was coming out of the kitchen to smoke a cigarette. She lived in the village and was not a member of the order. She seemed keen to speak to Conradin.

'You're new, aren't you?' she said, as she lit her cigarette and exhaled a small cloud of smoke.

Conradin nodded. 'I arrived last week,' he said.

'From the house in Salisbury?'

'Yes.' He was growing in confidence. Lying was so easy, he had discovered, even if it left you feeling uncomfortable.

The cook drew on the cigarette. 'I hear you've been doing wonders at the pig farm. Sister Gilbert said something about that. She said you've tarted the place up no end.'

'I do my best,' said Conradin.

'Like to come in for a cup of tea?' asked the cook. 'I've got some brewing.' She gave a toss of her head in the direction of the kitchen.

Conradin hesitated. He was wary of any new situation where he might be compromised, but the cook seemed friendly enough and her relaxed manner had put him at his ease.

'I should be getting on with my work,' he said, 'but ...'

The cook smiled. 'But all work and no play, Sister,' she said. 'You don't want Jack to be a dull boy.'

As they made their way into the kitchen, Conradin saw that there were two young women already there, sitting on chairs in front of a large, wood-burning range. One was conspicuously pregnant, the other less so. The young women looked up from the mugs of tea they were holding. They smiled at Conradin.

'This is Sister ... Sister ...' began the cook, looking for help from Conradin.

'Sister Conradin.'

'Ah, yes.' The cook gestured towards the young women. 'And this is Elsie, and her friend Minnie.'

Elsie, who was the older of the two, looked at Conradin in a frankly inquisitive way. 'Hello, Sister.'

Minnie mumbled something that Conradin did not catch.

'Elsie's one of our regulars,' said the cook. 'How many times have you been here, Else?'

Elsie grinned sheepishly. 'Four times, Mrs Evans.'

The cook turned to Conradin. 'You hear that, Sister Conradin? Four times. You'd think some people would learn from their mistakes.' She smiled. 'Not our Else!'

Minnie seemed keen to dissociate herself from this shamelessness. 'Not me,' she said. 'First time – last time.'

Conradin was not sure what to say. The whole exchange seemed good-natured – almost jocular – and yet, four times . . .

'I know I shouldn't,' said Elsie. 'But you know how fellows are.' She paused, and looked at Conradin. 'Of course, you nuns probably don't. It's hard for girls.'

'I'm sure it is,' said Conradin.

'A bit of self-control wouldn't go amiss,' said the cook.

This drew a response from Minnie. 'It's all very well for you,' she snapped. 'Married. Got a fellow who pulls his weight. Nice place to live. Yes, it's all right for you. Poor Else has none of that.'

'I've had to battle,' said the cook. 'I didn't get everything on a plate, I can tell you.'

Conradin was embarrassed, and the cook noticed this. 'We don't want to embarrass Sister,' she said. 'We can talk about these things some other time.'

'Yes,' said Elsie. 'There are lots of other things to talk about. There's the war, for instance.'

Conradin was silent.

'They say that careless talk costs lives,' said Minnie. 'You never know who might be listening.'

Elsie laughed. 'Are you saying Mother Superior could be a German spy? Is that what you're saying?'

'She could be,' said Minnie. 'How do you know she isn't?'

The cook intervened. 'They say they broke up a spy network in Norfolk the other day. They found ten radios hidden in a barn. All tuned to Berlin – every one of them. That's what they say.'

'Highly unlikely,' said Elsie. 'People exaggerate. The rumour mill, you know.'

'And you know what else they're saying,' the cook continued. 'They say that the Germans are dropping agents in dressed as nuns. I'm not making this up. Mrs Lewis at the post office told me about it. She said the police had been warning people to be extra vigilant.'

There was a sudden, awkward silence. Conradin felt his heart leap. He took a deep breath.

'Why would they do that?' he asked. His voice, he feared, sounded uneven. Would they notice?

'That's another of those rumours,' said Elsie. 'And it's probably the Germans who make them up. Lord Haw-Haw and the like.'

'They'll do anything, them Germans,' said Minnie.

Conradin finished the tea that the cook had poured for him. 'I have a long list of tasks,' he said.

'You nuns are always working,' said Minnie, grinning at Elsie. 'You don't have to, you know. You could stop and take it easy – like us.'

'Or some of us,' said Elsie, looking at Minnie with mock disapproval.

Conradin smiled. 'I'm sure you're both very busy – in one way or another.'

Elsie sighed. 'We know you don't think much of us, Sister. You don't have to be polite to us. We can take it.'

Conradin protested. 'But that's not true. I don't ...'

Elsie did not let him finish. 'We can't all be saints, you see.'

'No,' said Minnie. 'We can't. Remember Mary Magdalene.'

Elsie and Minnie looked at Conradin as if challenging him. But he simply said, 'Of course, Mary Magdalene.'

'She was a fallen woman,' said Elsie.

'Yes,' Minnie joined in. 'She fell.'

The cook nodded. She too was staring at Conradin. He cleared his throat. 'So much happened in the past,' he said. 'But times have changed.'

The cook looked puzzled, but then shrugged. 'I have some bread to bake,' she said. 'And you girls are meant to be helping me.'

'We must talk again some time,' said Conradin quickly.

Later, as they went into the refectory for dinner that night, Conradin mentioned to Sister Cecilia that he had met Elsie and Minnie. Sister Cecilia rolled her eyes. 'Those two,' she said. 'I don't know much about Minnie – she's only recently arrived. A respectable family, I believe. Somewhere up in Yorkshire. But that Elsie – we know her very well.'

'I hear she's a regular,' said Conradin.

'Four times!' whispered Sister Cecilia, under her breath. 'I don't like to be uncharitable, Sister Conradin, but frankly . . . four times.'

'And the babies?'

'They're in homes somewhere. I think they've kept them together. Obviously, adoption is a bit more difficult in wartime. Perhaps they'll place them when all this is over.' She paused. 'And different men, too. Four different fathers, would you believe it?'

Before he could express a view, Sister Cecilia continued, 'Mother is kindness itself, but I'm afraid Elsie has really tested the limits.'

Conradin shook his head. 'Oh well,' he said, 'every baby is a gift, I suppose.'

Sister Cecilia gave a snort. 'Four? Four gifts? No thank you, Sister.'

It was three weeks later that Sister Cecilia asked Conradin whether he would care to accompany her into Cambridge, which was not much more than an hour's drive away.

'Mother has asked me to collect some books from Heffers,' she said. She smiled. 'Improving literature. Somerset Maugham and E. F. Benson. Mother is a great reader and doesn't care much for the devotional stuff.'

Sister Cecilia explained that the convent owned a motorcycle, a BSA Blue Star, that was fitted with a sidecar. This had been on loan to the local vicar who was now returning it to the convent because he was unable to get the fuel to run it any longer.

'Mother has plenty of coupons,' Sister Cecilia explained. 'For everything. You name it, Mother has it. She's marvellous. She has plenty of petrol coupons.'

Conradin was intrigued. He wondered where Sister Cecilia had learned to ride a motorcycle. He asked her, and after only a few moments' hesitation she replied, 'Self-taught, Sister Conradin. That's the best way to learn to do anything. Teach yourself – then you really learn things well.'

'You obviously taught yourself well enough to get a licence,' observed Conradin.

Sister Cecilia looked shifty. 'There's the war, of course,' she said. 'These things are less important in wartime.' She assumed a business-like manner. 'We'll leave after Terce and be back in time for Nones, or certainly for Vespers.'

Conradin agreed, although not without some misgivings, and duly set off with Sister Cecilia the following morning, with Mother, Sister Gilbert, and Sister Angela waving good-bye at the front gate.

'Safe journey,' cried out Sister Angela, a small woman with an inordinately loud voice.

Sister Cecilia sounded the horn and Conradin waved. As they shot off down the road, he looked back over his shoulder at the three nuns standing at the gate, waving, and the thought crossed his mind that he had found a family. He had a family back in Germany, but he had created a family for himself here in England. Perhaps, he thought, that is what we all do in one way or another: create families for ourselves as we go through life.

The rural lanes were empty, apart from the occasional cyclist or a hurrying, preoccupied vehicle from the RAF base. They passed a horse and cart, the horse whinnying nervously at the sound of the motorcycle's engine. They stopped at a crossroads, where a bus bound for Cambridge was boarding a small knot of waiting passengers. One of these passengers pointed at them, and heads turned to take in the sight of two nuns sweeping past on a BSA and attendant sidecar.

In Cambridge they parked the motorcycle near the entrance to one of the colleges. Two undergraduates, fresh-faced, and dressed in white flannels and jerseys, smiled at them as they emerged from a low doorway. One doffed his striped cricketing cap, and was rewarded with a wave from Sister Cecilia and what looked like a mouthed kiss.

'Such sweet boys,' she observed, adding, 'such a pity.'

Conradin was not sure how to interpret this, and did not respond. He looked up at the sky, the wide sky of Cambridgeshire, and said, 'I've never been here before.'

Sister Cecilia said, 'I love the spires. The bridges. Everything.'

Conradin looked about him. How could anybody wish to destroy all this?

Sister Cecilia was looking at him. 'You look sad,' she said. 'Thinking of something?'

He hesitated, and then answered, 'Yes. I was thinking about the pointlessness of war.'

'You mean the evil?'

'Yes, that too.'

For a few moments they stood in silence. Then Sister Cecilia said, 'We should get along to Heffers. Then we can go and have tea in one of the tea-shops. Perhaps a scone as well. With jam.'

Conradin's delight on being in Heffers was such that Sister Cecilia suggested that she might leave him there and meet him later in the tea-room next door. She had one or two other errands to run in town, but she could do these herself while he browsed in the bookshop. He welcomed this suggestion, and they agreed that they would meet again at noon, two hours hence, when the planned tea and scone could become soup and a sandwich.

'Mother has given me some money,' said Sister Cecilia. 'She said that we can treat ourselves. She is so generous.'

'Yes,' agreed Conradin. 'Mother is very kind.'

'Mother is love,' Sister Cecilia continued. 'It does not matter who we are ...' And here she gave Conradin a meaningful look. 'No, it really doesn't matter who we are – Mother loves us in spite of ...' She paused, and the intensity of the look increased, '... in spite of *everything*.'

Conradin studied his fingernails. 'You're right,' he said. 'There are deep wells of love from which Mother draws.'

'Very deep,' said Sister Cecilia.

Conradin looked away. He had nothing further to say on the subject of Mother's love. He had said everything he wanted to on that particular subject. And so too, it seemed, had Sister Cecilia, as she now gave Conradin a little wave and wafted out of Heffers in a flurry of black and white. Conradin returned to his browsing, his eye running along the titles arranged on the shelf before him. There was so much that he wanted to read, so many books that he would dearly love to buy and take back to the convent with him in the BSA sidecar. He sighed.

He picked a book off the shelf. *The Poems of Matthew Arnold*. He held it in both hands before he opened it, remembering that the last time he had held this book was with a group of his students in Hamburg. There had been six of them, four young men and two women, and he wondered now what had become of them. The young men were probably caught up, just as he was, in the swirl of dire events that had consumed their world, pressed into the fight started by those shabby bullies in Berlin. Heaven knew where they would be – in the East, perhaps, facing unimaginable horrors – mired in misery, wherever they were. He wanted to weep for those young people, at the start – and possibly the end – of their lives. He had never done that, but now he wanted to, although he knew he could not – not here in Heffers Bookshop, holding a copy of *The Poems of Matthew Arnold*.

He had read 'On Dover Beach' to his students and now, as

he held it, the book fell open at that page. Others, perhaps, who had taken this particular volume off the shelf and had considered buying it, had turned to that most familiar of Arnold's poems.

He read it now, glancing about him lest anybody should overhear, whispering each word to himself, realising that whatever the poem had meant to him then, in Germany, it meant so much more now, in this place.

'Ah, love, let us be true
To one another! For the world, which seems
To lie before us like a land of dreams,
So various, so beautiful, so new,
Hath really neither joy, nor love, nor light,
Nor certitude, nor peace, nor help for pain;
And we are here as on a darkling plain
Swept with confused alarms of struggle and flight
Where ignorant armies clash by night.'

He replaced the book on the shelf. After the war, he said to himself, I shall come back here and buy this book, the very book. It would probably still be there, he felt, because at a time when nations were locked in conflict, when the world was in flames, there would probably be few people who would think of buying *The Poems of Matthew Arnold*.

He turned round. He was not sure what made him do so, but he felt that he had to turn. And as he did so, he saw the figure on the other side of the shop, completing a purchase at the cash desk. He drew in his breath. His hands clasped tight, as they might in a moment of great danger. He stood stock still.

He could not be mistaken; it was impossible. He could not be mistaken because he remembered so well the way that Johan Schneider had a way of standing, just so, and touching his cheek in that pensive gesture, which was what he was doing at that precise moment as he waited for the change from his purchase. It was him; it was Johan Schneider. It could be nobody but him: Johan Schneider, with whom he had spent those difficult four months of training in Hamburg; who came from a small village outside Cologne; who had been a trainee accountant; who played the trumpet, part-time, and not very well, in a dance band; who had a brother called Ferdi, who was a well-known long-distance runner; that Johan Schneider.

He almost called out. Absurdly, he almost called out across the room, forgetting everything – where he was, who he was – forgetting that he was in a nun's habit and Johan was in a dark, rather ill-cut suit of the sort worn by any number of office clerks. And if he had called out Johan's name, what would have happened? If Johan remembered his training he would pretend not to have heard and would certainly not reply. He might glance furtively across the shop floor, of course, and see a nun, but might not realise who the nun was. Unless he knew, that was; unless he had been told by Hamburg that Conradin Muller had disappeared and that he should look out for him in the area in which he had been dropped because he might be compromised by now. The British turned agents; they threatened them with execution unless they played along and sent misleading information back to Germany. The Abwehr knew all about that, of course, and would be cautious.

He waited. Johan had collected his change now, had thanked the bookseller, and was moving towards the front door. Conradin held back for a few moments, studying the spine of *The Poems of Matthew Arnold* in its place on the shelf. Then, as Johan left the shop he followed him at a discreet distance, out into the street and then down King's Parade, keeping sufficiently far away so that he should not be spotted but at the same time being close enough not to lose him. There were groups of students making their way to lectures; there were women out shopping; there was a file of choristers in the uniform of their calling; there were cyclists. Conradin kept his eye on Johan and remained with him as he went down a side street, along a busier road, down a shrub-lined path, and finally along a line of small terraced houses. Johan never looked back, which he should have done, had he been doing as their instructors had taught them. *Always remember to look behind you from time to time. And if you see the same person each time, then assume that you are being followed. Never walk anywhere without ascertaining whether you are alone.* And, of course, if you looked back and saw a nun trailing you, you should be doubly suspicious.

He sauntered past the house into which Johan had

disappeared, making a mental note of the name of the street and the number. Then, retracing his tracks, he made his way back into the centre of the town. He returned to Heffers and stayed there until it was time to meet Sister Cecilia in the tea-room.

'Did you have a good time in Heffers?' Sister Cecilia asked.

Conradin nodded. 'There are so many books I'd love to read. So many.'

'Yes,' said Sister Cecilia. 'Perhaps Mother will let you borrow her Somerset Maugham. Have you read any of his novels?'

He shook his head. 'I'd like to. People speak highly of him.'

The waitress came and took their order. They chose pea soup and cheese sandwiches. Ham sandwiches were available, but were twice the price of the cheese ones. 'Mother admires financial restraint,' said Sister Cecilia. 'And cheese is so nourishing.'

The waitress left.

'You spent the whole time in Heffers, then?' asked Sister Cecilia.

'Yes,' answered Conradin. 'The time flew by.'

Sister Cecilia looked up at the ceiling. 'I thought I saw you on the Parade.'

Conradin swallowed. 'Me? You saw me?'

'Well, unless it was another sister.' She paused. 'I was buying elastic. And a pair of new scissors for the girls to use to make those RAF pyjamas.'

For a few moments, neither of them spoke. Then Conradin said, 'Oh, that. Of course. Yes, I went for some air. Then I went back into Heffers. Bookshops can be so stuffy. Something to do with the paper, I think.'

Sister Cecilia's expression was impassive. Conradin looked away. 'I'm hungry,' he said.

The waitress appeared at the kitchen door and brought their soup and sandwiches to the table. They ate in silence at first. Conradin went over in his mind what he had said to Sister Cecilia. Had he sounded credible?

'I'd love to live in Cambridge,' Sister Cecilia said suddenly. 'It's such a vibrant place. Instead of being stuck out in the country, with the pigs and the fallen women, and . . . oh dear.'

'Perhaps you will, one day,' Conradin offered. 'You never know what life has in store.'

It doesn't have much in store for me,' said Sister Cecilia. 'Just the same thing. Matins. Breakfast. Pigs. Vegetables. Polishing. Vespers. And so on and so on.'

'But every life is like that,' said Conradin. 'Everyone's life has its routine. Mother's life. The Archbishop of Canterbury's life. Look at the king himself. What does he have in his day? Get up. Breakfast. Sign things. Pin medals on people. Afternoon tea. Dinner. That's it.'

Sister Cecilia laughed. 'You can be very funny, Sister Conradin,' she said. 'Is that your Icelandic sense of humour?'

'Possibly,' said Conradin. He thought of a rocky landscape, punctuated by geysers. He thought of green seas washing

46

against cliffs. He thought of how he might go somewhere, one day, anywhere where he might be free of the haunted dream into which the world had been tipped.

Sister Cecilia stared at him. Her face broke into a smile. Then she looked away, as if she felt she must end a dangerous moment of understanding, of intimacy.

They finished the meal and then, laden with a bag of books for Mother and another shopping bag that Sister Cecilia had filled with haberdashery, they made their way back to their motorcycle. A small group of students, sitting on the grass, watched in astonishment as they climbed onto the machine. Sister Cecilia waved to them gaily, and, embarrassed, they returned the greeting.

Sister Cecilia drove back erratically, narrowly missing a boy on a bicycle, and at several points almost leaving the road when she cornered too fast. Conradin did his best to avert disaster by transferring his weight in the sidecar when he felt it would help, but his relief on arriving back at the convent was palpable. They missed Nones but were in time for Vespers, at which it was Sister Cecilia's turn to read from the psalms, and Conradin listened as she spoke of those who would be like trees planted by the rivers of water. Their leaves would not wither, she said, and all that they did would prosper.

He felt her gaze fall upon him as she said this, and he knew, at that moment, that she knew. He was convinced now, and his conviction was confirmed as he glanced at Mother, who was also looking at him over her half-moon glasses, but who looked away quickly when she saw that he had noticed.

He felt strangely calm. It no longer mattered to him what happened. He was ready to give up. And with that willingness to surrender, there came a feeling of unexpected calm. He had done nothing wrong. He had never spied on anybody. He had never fired a shot in anger. He was a conscript in every sense of the word and it was never the fault of the conscript.

After Vespers the nuns all filed out of the chapel. Some of the fallen women had taken part in the service, as they occasionally did, and Conradin noticed Elsie and Minnie sitting modestly at the back. They smiled at him as he walked past with Sister Cecilia, and he returned their smile.

He returned to his room. Dinner would be served in the refectory an hour later, but Conradin decided that he was not hungry. When the bell announced the meal, he slipped out of his room and made his way to the chapel, which he now had to himself although a couple of candles had been left burning on the altar. English churches and chapels, Conradin had noticed, had a very particular smell – a slight mustiness that one encountered nowhere else. It must be a mixture of the odour of candle wax and ancient plaster and flowers left to wilt in the vase. It was a *quiet* smell, he thought – if smells can be quiet.

He found himself kneeling, his forehead pressed against the back of the pew in front of him. He closed his eyes and

waited for something to happen within him, although he
was not sure what that would be. In his mind's eye, now, he
saw Johan Schneider going through the door of that small
terraced house in Cambridge. He tried to rid himself of the
image, but it returned, and it brought with it the dilemma
that had been at the back of his mind throughout the return
journey from Cambridge and had persisted through Vespers,
pushing aside all thought of anything else. He knew that
there was an active spy in the heart of Cambridge. He knew
his address. What should he do?

He did not want Germany to win the war because he had
long since come to the realisation that his country was the
aggressor. This war was not England's fault, nor America's,
nor the fault of any of the others to whom it was causing
untold suffering. It was for this reason that Germany had
to lose. But Johan Schneider was, like him, just one person
caught up in a great conflict. He had never discussed with
him whether he had volunteered or been drafted – Johan had
never seemed to be interested in that sort of thing. He was
just there. So, he might have been every bit as reluctant a spy
as he, Conradin, was.

He could notify the authorities anonymously, so that there
would be no risk of compromising himself. They would act
on the tip – he had been told that they always did, no matter
that people were left right and centre falsely accusing their
neighbours of being enemy agents. And if they searched
that terraced house in Cambridge, he had no doubt but they

would find Johan's radio concealed there. Then all would be lost, and Johan would be tried and executed as a spy. That meant that the moment he disclosed what he knew, he would be starting a process that would lead to the death of somebody who, even although for a short time, had been a friend. Did he want to do that? Did he *have* to do that?

What if he did nothing? He imagined that Johan was sending back information on troop movements and the comings and goings at the air-force bases dotted around Cambridge. Every time he did that, he was doing something that could lead to the deaths of Allied servicemen. There was no getting round that brute fact. Johan was part of the war machine that threatened the very people amongst whom he, Conradin, had found sanctuary. He was not an innocent. He was a participant.

And yet he was also a man. He was a man who played the trumpet in a dance band, who had a brother called Ferdi, who doubtlessly was loved by a mother and aunts and a wife or girlfriend; who would not want to die. He was all that too.

He suddenly became aware that he was not alone. He did not move his head, but looked fixedly down at the kneeler below him. Whoever it was would think that he was deep in prayer and would leave him undisturbed. He did not want to engage with anybody.

It was Mother, and she now slipped into the pew beside him. He hardly dared look at her, but he saw her.

She whispered, 'I find you in prayer, Sister Conradin.'

He moved his lips. No sound came.

'I would normally not disturb a sister in her devotions,' Mother continued, her voice barely audible. 'But there are times when the presence of another helps the heart to be opened. And somehow, I think this is just such a time.'

Conradin said nothing. He heard his own breathing, though.

'You see,' Mother went on, 'sometimes people know what we think they do not know. Sometimes we believe that we are concealing the truth from others, but that truth has been grasped all along by the very people from whom we are so intent on concealing it.'

Conradin tightened his fists. If he were to flee, then this would be the time to do it. He could easily overpower Mother, substantial figure though she was. He could steal the BSA and be miles away by the time the authorities were summoned. He could go to ground. He could even go to that terraced house in Cambridge and join forces with Johan. He could lie about his radio. He could invent a story about having been unable to get in touch with Hamburg. He could save his skin – at least as far as his own side was concerned.

But then he realised that he did not want to do that, because that was not the sort of person he was and because that was not the side he was on. It was as simple as that.

He turned towards Mother.

'Mother,' he began, 'I am troubled in my heart.'

Her reply came quickly. 'Of course you are, my child. I can tell that.'

He caught his breath.

'I've known that, my dear,' Mother continued, her tone that of one explaining something very simple and obvious. 'I've been aware of that from the very beginning – from the time you joined us. I've been aware that there is . . .' She paused, and looked at him with such sweetness that he was emboldened to think that he could confess to her at that moment – and get away with it: somehow she would understand.

He was about to speak, but she interrupted him with a hand placed upon his forearm. He noticed the veins on her hand; her skin seemed almost translucent.

'My dear,' she said quietly. 'We all have our secrets. But there is one thing that has always been clear to me, and that is that the Lord is understanding.' She gave him another of her sympathetic looks. 'The Lord knows that it is not easy to be what you wish to be. And the Lord knows, too, that there are many good people who are obliged to be one thing when they might wish to be another. There is no harm in that.'

He listened. He was not sure that he understood.

Then she said, 'I know, you see.'

His every muscle tightened. He might have to act without delay. For a moment he thought he might even have to overpower Mother Superior in order to make his escape. But the thought appalled him: he could never hurt anybody, let alone this woman who had been so kind to him.

'And Sister Cecilia?' he asked. It was all he could think of to say.

'Oh, she knows too,' said Mother. 'She has always known. And Sister Gilbert too, but none of the others. We do not need to trouble the lesser sisters with burdensome knowledge.'

She smiled at him, and for a moment or two he wondered whether he had jumped to the wrong conclusion. When she said that she knew, *what* did she know? Perhaps she was thinking of something altogether different.

'I can see that you are surprised,' she said. 'But I have a good instinct for detecting disguise.' She smiled.

He looked at her incredulously. Was this all there was to it? Was that all that she knew?

'You see,' she went on, 'people make the wrong assumption. They think that somebody like me will not have any experience of the world. But I do, you know. *Nihil humanum mihi alienum est*, so to speak. I have, as one might say, seen it all.'

He relaxed. This was not nearly as bad as he imagined.

'Of course,' she continued. 'While you wear the habit of our order, you must be careful not to draw attention to yourself. Do you understand what I'm saying?'

'Of course, Mother. Of course I understand.'

Mother sat back in her pew. Her hands were folded on her lap. She looked utterly serene.

'You see,' she explained, 'Sister Cecilia followed you from Heffers. She had been observing you all the time, and when she saw you trailing that man, she assumed that you had guessed – as she had – that there was something suspicious about him. She put two and two together. She saw where he went, just as you did, and she informed me before Vespers. I informed the police and I believe that he has since been arrested.'

For the first time in this meeting, she looked disapproving. 'It was unwise of you to take that risk – no matter how well-intentioned you were. What if the police had become suspicious of you? We would all have been most embarrassed. I want you to reassure me that you will not do anything foolish.'

He sunk his head in his hands, and wept with relief. Mother put her arm about his shoulders.

He heard Mother's voice in his ear. 'We are all caught up in sad events that are not of our making. But such things should not rob us of our humanity or of the mercy and forgiveness that is our due. I don't want to know what unhappiness you are running away from. You are deserving of mercy, as much as I am, as much as any of our unfortunate young women are. You may stay with us until the end of this dreadful war. Your secret is safe.'

He could not speak.

'I think it might be best if you abandoned our habit now,' Mother continued. 'You may wear it in private, if that makes you happy, but not in public. We have an identity for you. You may become a Polish sailor who has been invalided out of the navy. You may grow a beard and dye your hair. Nobody will know.'

He looked at her in astonishment.

'Sister Gilbert has obtained papers from . . . from a friend of ours – from somebody who owes us a favour. You may move into the unoccupied cottage on the farm and be the manager of the piggery. You have been such a godsend to us on the farm – I hope you will continue to run it for us – but as a Polish sailor.'

He managed to say, 'Of course.' And then asked, 'And what will become of Sister Conradin?'

'We shall put it about that she has been called back to Salisbury,' said Mother. 'You will be concealed for a few days while your beard grows, and then you will appear and nobody will be any the wiser.'

He nodded.

'And I hope,' Mother continued, 'that you will be able to do something else for us in due course – should you wish to show any gratitude you may feel.'

'Mother,' he said. 'I shall do anything for you. Believe me – I shall.'

She inclined her head. 'Thank you,' she said. 'I shall remember that.'

Two days later Mother announced at dinner in the refectory that Sister Conradin would be returning to Salisbury the following day. Her presence in the convent would, she said, be sorely missed – particularly by those who had enjoyed relief from farmyard duties. That brought laughter. However, she was pleased to be able to impart the good news that in a couple of weeks they would be obtaining the services of a Polish sailor, invalided out of the navy, who would assume the duties of farm manager and general maintenance man for the convent. His name was Jan and Mother was sure that he would be welcomed by the entire community.

After his period of seclusion in a little-used attic room in the convent, Conradin was pleased to emerge as Jan. Sister Cecilia had obtained clothing for him, including a set of Polish navy blouses that were suitable for work on the farm and an all-weather smock of thornproof tweed. There were two pairs of new boots as well, and a chunky green sweater. She had made an effort, too, to make his farm cottage as comfortable and homely as possible, hanging new curtains that the fallen women made out of RAF pyjama material and exchanging a side of pork in the village for a newish bedroom rug.

Conradin relished his return to a masculine identity. He was happy in his cottage and in his work. He soon transformed the barns and made a start on replastering the chapel. Mother was extremely grateful.

He saw Elsie and Minnie from time to time. Elsie had taken to helping with the pigs, her undoubted maternal instincts being evoked by the large sow that had given birth to twelve piglets. The sow was anxious about people approaching her litter, but seemed to exempt Elsie from that suspicion. Minnie kept away from the pigs, but proved to be adept at mending fences, a task that she described as being not all that different from knitting, which she had always enjoyed.

One evening, Mother knocked at Conradin's door. She was bearing a large dish of apple crumble that she had made, and that she thought Conradin might appreciate. He invited her in, and put on the kettle for tea.

Mother looked about the kitchen. 'You have made this very homely,' she said.

'I do my best,' said Conradin.

She was watching him. Now she said, 'Of course, any house or cottage is much improved by a woman's touch, I always feel.'

Conradin grinned. 'I wouldn't argue with that,' he said.

'Perhaps one day you'll find somebody,' said Mother. 'Would you like that, do you think?'

Conradin hesitated. 'That is quite possible,' he said at last. 'I'm very happy here, you know.'

She watched him. 'Happiness is usually well-deserved,' she said quietly.

He made Mother a cup of tea. She thanked him, and began to sip at it.

'I've always hoped that Elsie would settle down,' Mother said. 'She's a very nice girl at heart, but she has ... well, she has her failings – just like the rest of us. What she needs, I think, is a bit of stability. A home. And, most importantly, a man.' She paused. The room was silent apart from the ticking of the kitchen clock.

Mother now continued, 'Yes, I've seen a lot of these fallen women – not that I approve of that term at all, mind you – but I have had a lot of experience of these young women and their needs. I think that Elsie is one of those girls who has certain urges that need to be met, if you see what I mean. If she had a man, and a place to stay, then I'm convinced she would settle down – as long as the man would be prepared to look after her needs, so to speak.'

Mother took another sip of her tea.

'In return,' she continued, 'the man would get a loving wife, a well-kept home, and, I am sure, plenty of children – if that was what he wanted. I expect there are men who would be quite happy with all that.'

She took another sip of tea. 'Particularly if Elsie came with a lifetime lease to a cottage – for example – just to name one thing.'

Mother stopped. She looked across the kitchen table at Conradin. He looked back at her. She was right – as she usually was. There were men for whom that would be not such a bad prospect at all.

'Of course,' Mother went on, 'Elsie is almost due. She would come with a baby. But every baby deserves to have a father, if at all possible, don't you agree, Conradin?'

He did.

Then she made a speech that caught him unprepared. It was something that he would think about for a long time, and about which he would never be certain.

'There are occasions,' she began, 'when we say something that is not entirely true. There are occasions when we do not reveal everything we know – when we know something else, for example, that could be very awkward for somebody, but choose not to say it. Instead, we say something that they think they understand, but that they have not really grasped.' She drew a breath. 'And then, of course, rather than make things difficult for somebody, we propose a course of action that will leave things undisturbed. And everybody is happier as a result.'

They were both silent for several minutes. She knows, thought Conradin. But then he thought: does she *really* know? No, he decided; she does not, and perhaps it is impossible to tell. But then he remembered something that Sister Cecilia had once said: 'Mother Superior is a tough old bird, you know. There's no fooling *her*.'

He did a quick calculation. He liked Elsie; he might even love her, if he allowed himself to. And there were worse fates than the one that Mother Superior was so clearly proposing.

'Mother,' he said at last. 'Do you think you might give me permission to marry Elsie?'

'That's a wonderful idea,' said Mother Superior, without hesitation. 'What on earth made you think of it? But of course, I – and all the other sisters – would be delighted.'

The wedding was attended by all the sisters and by a full complement of the fallen women.

'This was surely destined to happen,' said Sister Cecilia, as she congratulated the newly-weds outside the chapel.

'I think it was,' said Conradin, glancing at Mother Superior, who smiled back at him with her customary sweetness.

They had three children of their own, and the one that Elsie came with. Shortly after their wedding, Elsie's previous three were reunited with their mother and their half siblings. Mother provided the funds for an extension to the cottage. She was so thoughtful that way.

Syphax and Omar

1

Syphax Brahimi, espion

Imagine Algiers in 1924. Imagine an unforgiving North-African sun, with its concomitant short shadows, and its penetrating light. Imagine a working street in this city – a street of small shops, hidden arcades, and corners on which urchins stand, watching the business being conducted about them. There are no banks here, nor offices of any importance; no uniformed concierges, no elegant lines of palm trees. This is not a street on which people may saunter, admiring the clothing of others, discussing the displays in the shop windows. The people in this street, with the exception of the children, are on their way somewhere.

Now imagine two men walking along this street, one

behind the other. There is no traffic, and so they are unconcerned at being in the middle of the road. The man in the front is in mid-stride – a powerfully built man whose clothing marks him out as one who earns his living in an office rather than with his hands. He wears a fez at a slightly jaunty angle: this is a man who is aware of how he looks; not vain – just aware. He has a white shirt, a bow tie and a long frock coat. His name is Syphax Brahimi, and he is a spy by profession, although he derives almost half of his income as a *rentier*. Two of his five tenants have difficulty in paying the rent, but Syphax is a generous-spirited man and, unlike most landlords, he allows them time to pay, even when they have built up arrears. In return, his tenants express love for him – 'I never resent paying the rent to that man,' says one of them. 'When I am able to, of course.'

About ten paces behind him, wearing a white head-dress, is the figure of Omar Benamara. He, too, is a spy. He is poorer than Syphax, and he has eight children and a wife who will not talk to him, for fear, some say, of further children. Every time he tries to address her, she turns away from him, muttering incomprehensibly under her breath. She comes from a humble background – 'Her grandparents on one side were Kabyle from the mountains,' explains Omar. 'They were very difficult people – very independent, very opposed to the French. Opposed to everybody, actually.'

There is a figure standing in the shadows, watching

Syphax and Omar. This appears to be a woman, heavily veiled, but is, in fact, a man disguised as a woman. The disguise is generally ineffective, as the man is widely known in that part of the city as 'the man who is dressed as a woman but who is really a man'. This man is also a spy, thought to be working for the Comintern, but who also, when not dressed in his disguise, works as a receptionist in a small French hotel, *l'Auberge de Lyons*, three streets away. The only indication of his political sympathies is a small red badge that he wears on the lapel of his jacket when seated at the hotel's reception desk.

Syphax Brahimi is looking over his right shoulder. He knows that Omar has been following him, because that is Omar's job – just as his job is to follow Omar. Sometimes Syphax will be in the lead, and sometimes it will be Omar. The order depends on the day: on Mondays, Wednesdays and Thursdays Syphax will be followed by Omar; on Tuesdays, Saturdays and Sundays, Syphax will be trailing Omar. They may not be quite as regular in their street appearances as Immanuel Kant, but they are not far off. In Kant's case, the citizens of Königsberg could set their watches by the stages of the great philosopher's morning walk; the residents of Algiers are concerned only that Syphax and Omar should appear – they are largely indifferent to the timing of that appearance.

And imagine that there are two children in the background, watching the Comintern spy with all the innocent curiosity of the young. These children are a brother and sister. The sister is the older of the two. She is just seven. Her younger brother – aged three – many years later, in 1959, would be arrested. He had become an active member of the nationalist resistance to French rule. His political involvement put him in danger on several occasions, notably when he was picked up by a group of *OAS* men, beaten up and dumped in the harbour. They thought he was dead, but he was still breathing, and he floated. After independence he trained in massage and eventually became head masseur of the Algerian national football team. He was proud of what he had done with his life. He had two daughters who made good marriages, and an asthmatic son who went to Marseilles and became a taxi driver, eventually owning a fleet of three taxis.

All of that can be so easily imagined when one thinks of a street in Algiers in 1924. But of course there is much more in the lives of these two spies, Syphax and Omar, who were, in spite of being on opposite sides, great friends. Sides are often arbitrary – the result of historical accident: friendship can be much more important than allegiance and membership, and can, sometimes, outrank other, lesser loyalties. Where you are born, and the flag that flies over your birthplace, may turn out to be far less important than the promptings of the heart within.

2

Pantaléon Dubois, pied-noir

Syphax was born in 1876, the only son of the director of a trading company that exported dates and olives. As a young man, Syphax's father had nursed unfulfilled intellectual ambitions, and had, as a result, spared no expense in his son's education. At the age of seven, Syphax was placed under the care of a tutor named Pantaléon Dubois, an arrogant young French *colon* who resented being employed by an Arab-Algerian, but who needed the generous salary offered by Mr Brahimi. In spite of his assumptions of social superiority, Pantaléon proved to be an effective tutor. He not only insisted on hours of study of Racine, but he also gave Syphax a grounding in modern Greek. 'He might choose to live in Alexandria,' he explained to his employer. 'You never know, and it could be useful to him to have a knowledge of Greek.' Mr Brahimi nodded enthusiastically. 'I want my son to be a citizen of a broader world,' he said. 'I don't want him to think that the world begins and ends in Algiers. I'd like him to be able to go to Paris and mix with the people there – if he wishes, of course.'

Pantaléon said nothing. He resented the opportunities that would open up to Syphax. If anybody had the right to go to Paris and mix with educated circles there, then surely it was him, rather than this local upstart. But he knew that he could not afford to go to Paris and he knew, too, that there were people there who looked down on *pieds-noirs*.

Syphax had a retentive memory and an instinctive grasp of language. His French was near-perfect, and his Greek became passable, even if a bit halting. He enjoyed mathematics, but was not particularly numerate, which suited Pantaléon, for whom anything mathematical was an ordeal.

At the age of nineteen Syphax was summoned for a serious conversation with his father. 'I'm proposing to send you to Constantinople,' he said. 'I have been making enquiries and have found an academy there that specialises in the arts. It is called the Academy of Fine Arts and instruction is in French. They offer courses in art and music and in some of the lesser arts, such as glass-etching. They have informed me that there will be a place for you there in the next session, and I have accepted that – on your behalf.'

Syphax was silent.

'You're pleased?' asked his father.

'No,' said Syphax. 'I will always obey you, Father, as you are the fount of all wisdom. But I would very much prefer to go to Paris. You always talked about my going there – remember? You wanted me to meet intellectuals there. Monsieur Verlaine, for example. And other Symbolists. Remember?'

Mr Brahimi stared at his son. He shook his head. 'I have changed my views,' he said. 'I do not want my son mixing with Symbolists.'

'But Father ...'

Mr Brahimi's tone was firm. 'No, things are different. I have been told that Paris is now a very degenerate city,' he said. 'It is full of sexual perverts and women of low morals. It is not a place for a young man like you.'

Syphax listened to this denunciation of Paris. For all his father knew, he thought, he could himself be a so-called sexual pervert who enjoyed the company of women of low morals. But he did not say this, of course, and meekly agreed to go to Constantinople as his father wished.

'I shall work very hard at this academy,' he said to Mr Brahimi.

'I'm pleased to hear that,' came the reply. 'I shall give you a generous allowance and a good set of clothing to take with you. You will write to us once a month, please, and come back twice a year to see your mother.'

'I shall do all of that,' said Syphax.

3

A retired eunuch entertains

In Constantinople he took lodgings in a house owned by a middle-ranking official in the Ottoman bureaucracy, being allocated two rooms at the back of the rambling family home that the bureaucrat had inherited from a wealthy uncle. There were four rooms in this part of the house, the other two being occupied by one of the last eunuchs who had served in the Sultan's household. The eunuch was a large man with fleshy hands whose passion in his retirement was cooking elaborate dishes. He entertained friends in his living room, serving them his carefully prepared dishes and exchanging snippets of gossip late into the night. He knew everybody in Constantinople, it seemed, and kept a written record of the misdeeds and peccadillos of senior government servants. This, he said, was for the historical record. 'I have never sought to blackmail any of these people,' he said to Syphax. 'I am a chronicler of our times – that is all.' He paused. 'I am a chronicler of the weakness of others.'

Syphax enrolled at the Academy of Fine Arts and attended two weeks of classes there. The courses he took were *French Classical Art of the Eighteenth Century* and *Napoleon in Egypt*. The lectures on these subjects were delivered in a small auditorium, and were attended by no more than a handful of students. The lecturers were furtive in their manner, and Syphax was told by one of his fellow students that most of them were wanted by the police. One of them, a man described as the Professor of Aesthetics, never delivered his lectures himself, but sent his servant to deliver them for him. This servant did not actually speak French, but read out phonetically the script given to him by the professor.

After two weeks, Syphax stopped attending lectures.

Locating a printing office near the Pera Palace, he instructed the printer to produce stationery at the top of which the academy's name was printed. Underneath this, he had printed the words: *Student Monthly Report*, with a series of columns at the top of which subject headings were printed. At the bottom, there was a box entitled: *Student Conduct and General Disposition.*

Syphax collected this stationery from the printer and showed it to the eunuch. 'All I ask of you is that you fill this in for me,' he said. 'The academy is worthless and I hope to save my poor father the embarrassment of realising that he has made a bad choice.'

'You are a very considerate boy,' said the eunuch, and agreed to do as he was asked. He was, in fact, an expert forger, and had been trained in the alteration of documents in the department that the Sultan had established for those specific purposes.

At the end of the first month, a completed report was sent to Mr Brahimi in Algiers. In the box reserved for comments on conduct and disposition, the eunuch had written, in his florid cursive hand, 'This young man is a credit to his family. He is diligent in his studies and courteous to his professors. They all speak highly of him and believe that he has a very great future ahead of him. We recommend that he continue with his studies here for a further three years, after which he will be well-equipped to make his way in the world in whatever profession he chooses to follow. We also recommend a slight increase in his stipend to cover the rising cost of studying in this city.'

The eunuch read this out and then asked Syphax whether that would do.

'It is exactly what I had in mind,' said Syphax, 'although it would be helpful if you could change *slight* to *substantial*.'

'That will be no trouble at all,' said the eunuch, laughing as he applied his skills to the correction.

Syphax was happy in Constantinople. He quickly made a number of new friends whose company he found agreeable. He stayed in bed each day until eleven in the morning, when he would rise and saunter off to his appointment with his barber. Then he would have lunch with his friends and visit his favourite steam bath before returning to his lodgings in the late afternoon. On at least one or two evenings a week, he would be invited by the eunuch to join him and his friends over an elaborate meal and listen, entranced, to the gossip they exchanged. Soon he felt he understood exactly what was going on in the city. His Turkish quickly became fluent, although he was told that his accent verged on the effete. 'Charming, though,' said the eunuch. 'And these days, of course, an effete accent is considered very fashionable.'

Three years passed. Syphax never returned to the Academy of Fine Arts, although he continued to send forged progress reports to his father. There were no home visits to Algiers, as he claimed to be working too hard, and his father accepted the excuse. 'You can never work too hard,' he wrote back. 'That's the way to get ahead in life.'

Life in Constantinople suited Syphax very well. Nothing much happened, beyond meetings with friends and trips to restaurants and the baths. You could live such a life for ever, he thought, and not get bored with it. And that, he decided, was what he would do.

4

Nercessian, Armenian

It was through the eunuch that Syphax first met a member of the Ottoman Secret Service. This was a thin-faced Armenian whose walrus moustache was stained yellow with nicotine. He was an old friend of the eunuch, who explained that they had once visited Cairo together. They both enjoyed playing chess, although the eunuch complained that his friend was inclined to cheat if he was not watched closely. 'It's his training,' he said. 'He's a spy, you see. They train them to do things like that and it becomes second nature. Never play any game of chance with those people – they cannot help themselves. They will cheat every time.'

The Armenian was called Mr Nercessian. 'I know it sounds like *narcissist*,' he said to Syphax. 'But I am not a narcissist. I do not like to look in mirrors.'

'That's because you have done such dreadful things,' joked the eunuch. 'Only the innocent can look at themselves in a mirror ...' He pointed at Syphax, a fond, even complimentary gesture. 'Innocents like Syphax here.'

Mr Nercessian smiled, and winked at the eunuch. The eunuch returned the wink but then, when he saw that the exchange had been intercepted by Syphax, assumed a serious expression. Syphax found himself wondering about the nature of the relationship there between the spy and the eunuch. Was it a simple friendship, or was he missing something? The eunuch's friends, as far as he had been able to observe on the occasions on which he had been invited to join them, were conventional in their dress and manner. None of them, he thought, was a eunuch, and most spoke of homes and families that were, from the references they made to them, unexceptional in their ordinariness. Admittedly, one or two of them were unusual – the eunuch was friendly with a dwarf who played in a palm court orchestra and whose life, Syphax suspected, was unconventional. And there was another friend who was, according to a comment made by Mr Nercessian – in an unguarded aside – a dealer in stolen horses; but he was an exception to the progression of minor bureaucrats constituting the bulk of the eunuch's circle. Perhaps the appeal lay in the kitchen, as the eunuch himself had once suggested: 'They like me,' he confided, 'because I feed them so well when they come round here. It's like feeding stray cats – they like you if you give them something good to eat. That's the basis of friendship, you know, Syphax. Don't delude yourself that it's all about shared interests and noble ideals. It's food. Or money. Money is a wonderful maker of friends. If you have money, you have friends.'

Now Mr Nercessian responded to the eunuch's remark about innocence. 'If Syphax is so innocent, then he should consider joining us. Innocence is always a good cover in intelligence work.'

Syphax said nothing at first, but then, a few minutes later, when the conversation had moved on to a discussion of Russian intentions, he brought up the subject of espionage. 'You said I would make a good spy, Mr Nercessian. Do you really think so?'

Mr Nercessian turned to face him. The Armenian was eating a large rosewater cake that the eunuch had made, and he popped the rest of this into his mouth before licking the crumbs off his fingers. 'I'm quite sure you would,' he said. 'Spies are born, not made. I detect in you just the right attitude – the right intuitions.' He paused. 'I could sound out my superiors, you know. Would you like me to do that?'

Syphax hesitated. He was aware, somewhere deep within him, that the answer he gave to this question would shape the rest of his life. In this respect he was fortunate: it is often the case that when we are placed in such a position, we do not realise the significance of the answer we are about to give, and therefore dictate the shape of our future without being aware of what we are doing.

'Well?' prompted Mr Nercessian.

Syphax glanced at the eunuch, who shrugged.

'Yes,' said Syphax. 'I would be most grateful, Mr Nercessian, if you were to speak to your superiors in those terms.'

'You must be getting bored,' said the eunuch. 'A young man has to do something. You can't spend your time going to the barber and sitting around at the baths.'

Syphax looked away in embarrassment. 'I am very willing to work,' he muttered. 'I am not lazy. I haven't been doing much over the last few years because I have been busy thinking about what I should do in the future. You shouldn't rush these decisions.'

Mr Nercessian lit a cigarette. 'I'm sure you're not lazy,' he said. 'And I'm sure you will do very well in my profession. There are many opportunities.'

'My profession was far safer,' said the eunuch. 'But alas, there are few openings in it these days.' He looked sad. 'It used to be different, of course. We were very influential.'

'Everything is changing,' said Mr Nercessian. 'All this talk of freedom. All this undermining of the empire. First the Greeks, and now, heaven knows who will be next.'

The eunuch sighed. 'I shall now serve a very special course,' he said. 'This is lamb cooked for two days in a sauce for which only I and one or two other people know the recipe. There are twenty-two spices involved, some of them being unavailable to the general public. You will like it very much.'

Mr Nercessian now turned to Syphax. 'I take it you will be

prepared to study? You will need to attend our special college for at least a year. All your expenses will be met, of course.'

Syphax answered that he would be happy to do this.

'In that case,' said Mr Nercessian, 'my conversation with my superiors will be not much more than a formality. You may take it that you will be accepted.'

'You see,' said the eunuch. 'That's the way to do things.'

Syphax began his studies at the Ottoman Secret Service College two weeks later. The cadets, as the students were called, wore blue uniforms with silver rings on the sleeves and the words *Secret Service* emblazoned on the chest of their tunics. Syphax thought it rather strange that what should be secret should be so openly proclaimed, and he raised the matter – courteously – with the college principal. The principal listened to what he had to say and then simply put a finger to his lips and said, 'Hush.' Nothing more was said, and Syphax left the office. Mentioning this later to Mr Nercessian, the spy laughed and said, 'That's all he ever says. I remember, he was on the staff when I was at the college a long time ago. He did exactly the same thing then. Anything you said to him was greeted with a finger to the lips and the word *Hush.*'

Syphax completed the course with distinction. At the end of the year he was fully trained in techniques of shadowing, in communicating using dropped messages, and in the art of interrogation. He also learned how to don a disguise, how to assess psychological weakness in others, and how to use invisible ink. At the end of the course, Syphax was placed third in the list of graduates, a position that resulted in his beginning his first attachment on the third rung of the salary scale. He was very pleased, and wrote to his father to tell him that he had completed his course at the Academy of Fine Arts in record time and was now taking up employment in the Ottoman Civil Service. The eunuch forged a graduation certificate from the Academy of Arts and this was sent to Mr Brahimi, who framed it and displayed it proudly in his office. 'That's not worth the paper it's printed on,' said Pantaléon scathingly when he came to visit the house. 'It's rubbish.'

'You're envious,' said Mr Brahimi. 'Get out of my house immediately.' Then he added, 'One day my people will rise up and shoot all of your people. That's one hundred per cent certain, you know.'

5

Aristotle, agent

Syphax started his career as an Ottoman spy shortly before the turn of the century. He was then twenty-three, having spent three years pretending to be a student at the Academy of Fine Arts and a further nine months learning his trade of espionage. For the first year of his service, he was allocated to a department that filed reports – a job he found mind-numbingly boring. After a month of doing this, and feeling desperate, he revealed his dissatisfaction and frustration to Mr Nercessian, when he met him for dinner one evening in the eunuch's rooms.

'The worst thing,' he complained, 'is trying to file reports that have been written in invisible ink.'

'Operational reasons,' interrupted Mr Nercessian. 'Some agents have to use invisible ink because of their situation.'

'I know that,' said Syphax. 'But when they get to me, what do I do with them? How can I tell what they're about?'

'Have you ironed them properly?' asked Mr Nercessian. 'It's the ironing that reveals the writing.'

'Yes, I always iron them,' said Syphax. 'But it doesn't seem to work.'

'Then file them under *miscellaneous*,' said Mr Nercessian. 'That's what I used to do.' He paused. 'But you're really unhappy? Is that correct?'

Syphax nodded. 'I can't face years of this. They told me I might be in that department for five years. I can't face that.'

'And you've done a month so far?'

Syphax nodded. 'Of course, I've taken eight or nine days off,' he said. 'I had to go to the barber, you see. And I had an ingrowing toenail.'

Mr Nercessian winced. 'Painful. Entirely justified. You can't work with an ingrowing toenail.' He paused. 'There is a solution, you know.'

Syphax waited. He noticed that Mr Nercessian had

lowered his voice – a habit of his when saying anything remotely important.

'Many people take what I might call a pragmatic view of this sort of thing.'

Syphax raised an eyebrow. 'Yes?'

'Yes. They employ somebody to do their job for them. You pay – and it needn't be very much – for some poor fellow to pretend to be you. He goes in and does your work for you, and nobody's any the wiser.'

Syphax remembered the professor who had detailed his servant to deliver his lectures for him. He told Mr Nercessian about this, and the older man nodded. 'That's widespread in colleges and universities. Also, in some hospitals, I'm afraid, which is a bit more concerning. There are some very successful surgeons who never have to operate on patients – because they employ actors to do the job for them. They claim to give them a bit of training that serves them for most simple procedures. For more serious ones, they employ medical students keen to make a bit of money.'

'Could you arrange for somebody to do my job?' asked Syphax.

Mr Nercessian thought for a few moments. 'I have just the man,' he said. 'He even looks a bit like you, which is helpful. He has debts and he'll be pleased to earn the money. You could take him on for a year or two.'

Syphax expressed his gratitude. 'That will be a great help,' he said.

'And in the meantime,' Mr Nercessian continued, 'I've been thinking of offering you a job myself.'

Syphax was interested. 'Doing what, Mr Nercessian?'

'My job,' he replied. 'I want a bit of a break. You could do my job, which consists of following people. That would enable me to pursue my private interests a bit more. I'll pay you well enough. And it'll enable you to get out and about more often.'

Syphax smiled. 'That would suit me very well.'

Mr Nercessian hesitated. 'There's something I should add,' he said, lowering his voice yet further. 'Most of the suspects I follow . . . Well, they don't actually exist. I've found it simpler to invent them, if you see what I mean.'

'You make them up? Entirely?'

Mr Nercessian smiled. 'Well, some of them are based on real people – but people who have died. It's safer that way. Others are figments of my imagination – but very credible characters, I must say. The point is filing reports, you see. What they – the powers that be – want is lots of reports. What difference if the reports are about people who don't actually exist? The important point is that the authorities are confident they have the situation under control. And if the authorities feel they have the situation under control, then everybody can get on with the rest of their business in peace.'

'Which leads to happiness all round?'

'Precisely. All you have to do is to file reports. One in ten of them will be read by somebody more senior, and so you have to do it credibly. But as long as you do that, you'll be all right.'

Mr Nercessian lit a cigarette, using a gold lighter that Syphax had noticed bore the initials of another. Those of a victim? But the Armenian was too cultivated, too courteous to do anything crude. Perhaps he had found it somewhere and had decided to hold on to it: even a spy might hesitate to have unduly close contact with the police, even with their lost-property department.

'Of course,' Mr Nercessian continued, 'you don't want to keep your suspects going for too long. Give them a couple of years and then report that they've gone into exile. That usually pleases the authorities. And it enables you to start again.'

'Very satisfactory,' said Syphax.

'Yes,' said Mr Nercessian. 'The best of all possible worlds, as our friend Dr Pangloss might say.' He smiled. 'One of my suspects is actually called Pangloss. I gave him the name. It suits him.' He paused. 'He's just gone into exile, actually. I've replaced him with a Mr Aristotle, who's meant to be a Greek agent.' He grinned. 'And you know what those idiots in Head Office said? They said, "Watch this Greek, this Aristotle. We think he might be trouble. We've heard the name somewhere."'

The eunuch, who had been listening to this conversation with amusement, shrieked with laughter.

'Rich!' he exclaimed. 'If ever there was an empire destined to fall, it's this one.'

*

Time, languid even in those mellow, shaky years of the Ottoman Empire, passed agreeably slowly. Syphax spent the period between 1900 and 1904 in Constantinople, employed by the Ottoman Secret Service, doing Mr Nercessian's job between daily visits to the coffee houses and baths, and occasional lunch parties on the shores of the Bosphorus. The eunuch gave him regular cookery lessons, and in 1903 Syphax helped him to establish a small cookery school for the daughters of wealthy officials. Even traditional parents were happy to allow these young women to be tutored by a eunuch, and his courses were soon over-subscribed. 'One day,' he remarked to Syphax, 'it might be possible to teach young men how to cook. That will not be for many years – probably not in our lifetimes – but it will happen, I think.'

In 1904 Mr Nercessian was informed that he was to be sent on service abroad. This brought consternation, as he had developed business interests in Constantinople that would suffer if he were to leave them in the hands of unreliable managers. 'I must ask you to repay the favour I did you,' he said to Syphax. 'I must ask you to take this assignment in my place. I can arrange for a forger to delete my name from the relevant departmental minute and insert yours in its stead. That is all that will be required. It's a very common procedure.'

Syphax realised that he would have to comply. Favours were a serious business in the Ottoman Empire, and by any standards he was heavily indebted to Mr Nercessian.

'Where is this posting?' he asked. 'I'm not saying I won't do it, but I would just like to know where I am to be sent.'

'You're in luck,' said Mr Nercessian brightly. 'It is to Algiers. Can you believe that? This is something sent by the Almighty. It is clearly meant to be.'

Syphax sighed. It was bound to happen, and he would simply have to reconcile himself to it. Sooner or later, the place where you are destined to be will come and claim you. It always does. You may think you've escaped, but you never have: like gravity, such places pull you back, assert their control of your life. You won't get away from us that easily, say these places. We are your place; this is where you are destined to die, however long your life may prove to be. Don't fight it; submit, and in your acceptance you may find peace and contentment. Many do.

6

They followed

Syphax was welcomed back into the bosom of his family by his father, who embraced him warmly, tears streaming down his face.

'I knew you would return,' he sobbed. 'I knew you would never abandon us.'

'Such a thought never crossed my mind, Father. Not once.'

'And all those years of studying,' Mr Brahimi went on. 'Now you are an educated man – capable, I'm sure, of holding your own in the presence of anybody Paris can come up with. Anybody.' He paused. 'But what do you actually do, Syphax? What's this job of yours with the Ottomans?'

Syphax hesitated, but then, holding himself erect, he said, 'I'm a spy, Father. I'm an Ottoman spy.'

Mr Brahimi's eyes widened, but only momentarily. Then he let out a guffaw of laughter. 'Of course. Of course, you're a spy. That's the best cover for being something else. I understand. You say you're a spy, but in fact you're an official in the Ministry of Supply, or in some such post. It's very cunning.'

Syphax shook his head. 'No, Father, you have it wrong. People have mundane-sounding jobs as cover for their real jobs as spies. You have it the wrong way round.'

Again, Mr Brahimi laughed. 'You're not going to fool me that easily,' he said. 'You can't hoodwink your own father.'

Syphax abandoned any attempt to explain the situation to his father, and settled into his new posting. His instructions were to open an office in Algiers and to observe the doings of the various exiles – republican dissidents and reformers who had sought sanctuary there. He was given a generous budget for the payment of informers, an entertainment fund, and an allowance for the purchase of clothing.

Syphax had no interest in pestering the exiles, for whom he had considerable sympathy. Indeed, he went even further than simply abstaining from bothering them – he sent in false reports to Constantinople detailing the imagined demise of various opponents of the regime: two were reported drowned at sea, another was said to have been attacked by a rabid dog and have succumbed to hydrophobia, and several were poisoned. The exiles were real, and remained alive and well, but Constantinople was delighted to hear of their trials and tribulations. In respect of the exile reported to have been bitten by a rabid dog and to have developed hydrophobia, Headquarters in Constantinople sent a coded telegram to Syphax asking him to confirm that the poor man had suffered an agonising death. 'Can confirm death very agonising,' Syphax replied.

The false reports on the death of the exiles had the effect of relieving them of anxiety. Since they were now officially dead, and their names removed from the list of those of interest to the regime, the exiles could relax their vigilance. Although Syphax never spoke to them directly, the exiles became aware of just who it was who had done them the favour of killing them off, and responded by establishing a credit balance for his benefit at Syphax's regular restaurant, *la Maison de St Julien*.

But reports had to be written, and so Syphax decided that he would devote his time to what he described as his 'counter-intelligence' initiative. This involved following the prominent spy, *bon viveur* and chess champion, Omar Benamara. Omar, who was roughly Syphax's age, was a spy for the Italian government, which although not directly involved in Algerian affairs was interested in what was happening there on the grounds that Algeria was adjacent to its claimed zone of influence in Libya. Omar had been recruited to keep an eye on any agents of other powers who might have an interest in Italian ambitions. This meant that Syphax, as a spy for the Ottomans, who were the current rulers of Libya, was of interest. In a dispatch to Rome, Omar warned them that Syphax needed to be watched constantly as he was in regular touch with the Ottoman authorities in Tripoli and could be expected to do whatever he could to flout Italian claims to be the stabilising power in Libya itself.

The result of this was that Syphax and Omar came to spend every day following one another, moving from café to café, waiting to see exactly whom the other was meeting. They soon became aware of each other, and although they did not speak in the earlier days of this arrangement, they acknowledged one another's presence with a courteous nod of the head.

In 1923, with the emergence of the Republic of Turkey, Syphax was assumed as an employee of the new government. He and Omar continued to trail one another, noting down each other's movements and sending reports back to Rome and Istanbul. They now exchanged a few friendly words in the cafés they frequented, although they still maintained separate tables. The one exception to that rule was on the birthday of either of them, when a single table allowed them to share the birthday cake that the proprietors of the cafés would bake for them. As he sampled these cakes, Syphax invariably cast his mind back to the eunuch and the rosewater cakes he made in Constantinople. 'I once knew a eunuch who made delicious cakes,' Syphax said to Omar. 'That was long ago, though, in a world that seems to have passed . . .'

'Oh,' said Omar.

Syphax retired in June, 1935, shortly before his sixtieth birthday. Omar retired two months later. Neither could bear the thought of abandoning their routine, and so they continued to follow one another, as they always had done, through the streets of Algiers, keeping a short distance behind whoever was in front, employing all the usual tricks of disguise and shrugging off that they had acquired in their early training.

They appreciated one another. 'Omar is a true professional,' Syphax said. 'We shall not see his like again.'

'Syphax is a great spy,' Omar reciprocated. 'In the history of intelligence, there have been few of his calibre.'

When Syphax turned sixty-five, Omar gave him a book on the history of Turkish ceramics. The world was then at war. Syphax said, as they sat in a café and read the news from Vichy, 'It's so different from our own day, isn't it?'

Omar agreed. 'Ours used to be a gentlemanly profession.'

'You're right,' said Syphax, a note of sadness in his voice.

They finished their coffee. Then Syphax rose to his feet and left the café. Omar followed him.

Ferry Timetable

His name was Fergus Andrew Mactavish and he was a farmer in a remote part of Argyll. He went to his grave, unexposed, in 2003. At that simple ceremony of farewell, conducted under a West Highland sky filled with sharp, April light, only two of those present were aware of any claim that Fergus might have to be listed in the company of some of the century's best-known spies. And those two would never speak about it. Never.

Mactavish – as he was generally known – had a farm not far from Ardgour, a village on the shores of Loch Linnhe, a long sea loch that led up to Fort William and the Great Glen beyond. Ardgour did not consist of very much – a hotel, well-placed at the top of the ferry slipway, a general shop, and a post office. But that was all that most people needed. For any other purpose there was Fort William a brief ferry ride and drive away, or Oban about an hour or so further south. Above the village there were great sweeps of mountainside down which, after heavy rain, thin waterfalls fell like white threads. It was dramatic scenery by any standards, but taken for granted, as such things always are, by those who lived there. The mountains, though beautiful, supported very few sheep; the waterfalls and lochs were all very well but they led to the general damp that brought the midges in their summer swarms; and the sea loch cut one off from places that would otherwise have been more easily reached. Yet it was clearly far better than Glasgow, where people went off in search of work, only to find that they yearned for everything they had left behind, and from which they often returned, determined not to leave again.

Mactavish's farm was barely two hundred acres, but was large enough to support a small herd of beef cattle and a flock of Blackface sheep. He was a good farmer, and made the most of things, as had his wife, who had died when their daughter, Kirsty, was seventeen. Kirsty remained at home, not entirely out of a sense of duty, but because she saw no reason to go anywhere else. This suited Mactavish, as she was a good housekeeper, but he occasionally wondered what would happen if she were to marry. He hoped that she would do so, of course, as he wanted her to be happy, and he belonged to a generation where to be single was seen as a failure significantly reducing one's chances of happiness. But she showed no signs of looking for a husband, smiling enigmatically whenever he tactfully mentioned the possibility. 'You never know,' she said. 'Maybe I will, maybe I won't.

And there aren't all that many decent men around here, if you ask me. So maybe I won't.'

In 1980, when Mactavish was fifty-four and Kirsty was twenty-seven, there was a major crisis in their household. This concerned land and came about when the local council declared its intention of slicing off a portion of Mactavish's best field in order to build a new road.

'Nobody needs a new road,' Mactavish pointed out in a long and outraged letter to his councillor.

'Probably not,' replied the councillor. 'I certainly voted against it, but it's the committee, you see. They're the ones who look after roads and things like that. They said we do need a road, and that's that. You'll get your compensation, remember.'

That, thought Mactavish, was not the point. He wanted land, not money, and he vigorously protested his case to this effect, even engaging a solicitor in Inverness to write on his behalf to the council. His efforts were to no avail, though, and he concluded that the British state, as represented by its road-making authorities in the Western Highlands, was rotten to the core.

Tossing and turning in his bed one night, filled with resentment at the imminent arrival of the council's bulldozers, it occurred to him that if the authorities could treat a law-abiding farmer in such a way then they had sacrificed any claim they might have to his loyalty. And it was at that point, just as he was about to get up to attend to the livestock, that he decided he would work for the Soviet Union. That would teach them, he thought. That would teach them up in Inverness. That would teach them in Edinburgh and London. They would have only themselves to blame.

The *Oban Times* had reported in considerable detail the exposure of Anthony Blunt, and Mactavish was amongst those readers who had followed the case with some interest. He had read about controllers and meetings in London parks. He had read about the Soviet Union's seemingly insatiable appetite for information about military arrangements; well, he thought, Loch Linnhe was a waterway of some importance: you could take a submarine up as far as Fort William if you really wanted to, and that, in fact, might be just the sort of thing that the Soviet Union might wish to do. The *Oban Times* had once reported Russian submarines being sighted off Skye, and that was not all that far away. If you were prowling around Skye in a submarine then it might be quite convenient to be able to slip into Loch Linnhe for a day or two and rest while British submarines looked for you in the Sound of Mull. You would have to be careful, though, that you didn't try to cross the route taken by the Corran Ferry, because the loch was not all that deep at that point and the last thing you'd want would be for your conning tower to be clipped by the ferry's propeller.

Mactavish thought about all this, and then, in a sudden moment of decision, he obtained a copy of the Corran Ferry timetable. This he placed in an envelope with a covering note, and, having obtained the address of the Soviet Embassy in London from a telephone directory in the Fort William Public Library, posted it. The covering note said: *I am prepared to work for you. This information could be helpful for submarine activity. Please contact me for further assistance. Yours truly, F.A. Mactavish.*

Kirsty noticed that her father seemed somewhat jumpy over the days that followed. He had not mentioned his act of treason to her, of course, and she had no idea why he showed such interest in the arrival of the postmistress in her van.

'Are you expecting something?' she said. 'A cheque maybe?'

Mactavish shook his head. 'No,' he said. 'Nothing.' Even as he spoke, the thought crossed his mind: *How very easy it is to lie. That's what those people did. Philby and the others. They were very good liars.*

After a week of waiting, he began to feel anxious. What if the letter had been intercepted by the authorities? What if the intelligence people in London had steamed it open and found the Corran Ferry timetable and his offer to work for the Soviets? He had put his address at the top of his letter and so they would have no difficulty tracing him. Perhaps that was a mistake. Perhaps he should have arranged a meeting at what the *Oban Times* had described as a 'drop-off point'. He swallowed hard. *I'm an amateur*, he thought. *I've made the most fundamental of mistakes.*

The sense of excitement and anticipation that he had felt

was now replaced by a gnawing sense of dread. This was compounded by guilt. He had betrayed his country in a fit of anger and now, on more mature reflection, he realised what a terrible thing he had done. His father had served in the Argyll and Sutherland Highlanders, just as his grandfather had done. An uncle had been in the Black Watch and had been commended for his bravery. And here he was, Fergus Mactavish, offering his services to the Soviet Union, about which he knew nothing and which had no claim at all on his loyalty.

He went to see the local Church of Scotland minister. Sitting awkwardly in the minister's study, a cup of tea cooling at his elbow, he confessed what he had done. The minister allowed him to tell the whole story before he said anything.

'You should drink your tea, Mactavish,' he said at last. 'I can't take cold tea myself – never could.'

There was a brief silence. Then the minister continued, 'You sent them the ferry timetable, you say?'

Mactavish nodded miserably.

The minister smiled. 'I wouldn't worry too much about that, you know. You can get the ferry timetable in the shop.'

'But I offered to do more.'

The minister raised an eyebrow. 'What else could you do? I'm not being rude, but what on earth could you do for the Soviet Union?'

Mactavish stared at the floor. 'You don't think it's too bad?'

The minister shook his head. 'Come on, man, be sensible! Anybody who heard about this would burst out laughing.

Anybody would think it's a great joke. Nobody would take it seriously.'

Mactavish left the minister's house feeling as if a great weight had been taken off his shoulders. He returned to the farm, where he made a full confession to his daughter.

'I knew there was something biting you,' she said. 'But I had no idea it would be so ridiculous.'

Mactavish said nothing. He wanted now to forget all about it. It was coming up to the lambing season and he would have his hands more than full with that.

A month later, a letter arrived from the Soviet Embassy. When Mactavish opened it and saw the headed paper, he gave an involuntary gasp. His daughter, who had just come into the room, looked at him with concern.

'Is that about the road?' she asked.

He handed the letter to her. 'It's from the Russians,' he said. 'They're coming to see me.'

She frowned as she read it. 'So this Mr Yuri Olevsky is coming next week,' she said. 'Well, you just go to the police. Speak to Sergeant Cameron.'

'I can't do that,' Mactavish exclaimed. 'I can't go and tell the police that I offered to work for the Soviet Union. Willie Cameron would have to arrest me. I'd be taken off to Inverness Prison before I knew what was happening.'

Kirsty thought for a moment. 'But they might *turn* you. MI5 or whoever they are might use you as a double agent.'

Mactavish dismissed this suggestion. 'This is what happens

when you do what I did,' he said, his voice full of misery. 'It's the same as with that fellow, Blunt. You get in too deep and then you can't get out again.'

She took her father's hand and held it. He looked at her, lovingly, in gratitude. Family would always forgive; they would forgive wrongs both small and large; meanness, venality, even treason.

'When Mr Olevsky comes,' she said quietly, 'we'll give him a cup of tea but we must be firm. We shall tell him that you are no longer prepared to serve the Soviet Union.'

'I don't think I ever really began to do that,' said Mactavish. 'That's what the minister said.'

'Well, there you are,' said Kirsty. 'You can tell him that you're not going to start.'

She looked out of the window. A squall had blown in from the south west – a veil of gentle rain, like white mist, moving across the surface of the distant loch. The light behind it had the quality of silver.

Yuri Olevsky was in his early thirties – rather younger than they had imagined. He had dark, slicked down hair, which lent him the appearance of a 1930s dance instructor. He had very white teeth, and regular features. He was very handsome.

They drank tea together. He seemed nervous, and after a few minutes of pleasantries, Mactavish thought that he should not delay in revealing his change of heart.

'With all due respect to the Soviet Union,' he said, 'I have decided that I do not wish to get involved.'

Olevsky looked at him. 'This place you have here is very beautiful,' he said.

Mactavish inclined his head in recognition of the compliment.

Then Olevsky said, 'I am ashamed of my country. I, too, no longer wish to serve it.'

Mactavish and his daughter stared at him. Neither knew what to say. Treason, it seemed, unknown in Ardgour since the 1745 Jacobite rebellion – and that wasn't real treason, if you were a Jacobite – now seemed endemic.

Eventually Mactavish found his voice. 'Oh,' he said. And then he added, 'Aye.'

'I told my superiors that I was following up a lead in Glasgow,' Olevsky continued. 'They do not know I am here.' He paused. 'I should therefore like to apply for political asylum.'

Mactavish looked at Kirsty. 'What do we do?'

Olevsky intercepted the question. 'You fetch the authorities,' he said.

Mactavish shrugged his shoulders. 'We don't have any authorities up here. There's Willie Cameron, I suppose, but he's not based here. He's at the police office in Strontian.'

Now Kirsty acted. 'Why don't you just stay with us?' she asked. 'You could get work in the hotel – the one down by the ferry. And I know somebody who's looking for someone to help him on his fishing boat.'

Mactavish opened his mouth to protest. She had not asked him how he would feel about having a Russian staying in the house, but then he stopped himself. He looked at his daughter; she was gazing at Olevsky, who was smiling back at her encouragingly.

Over the three weeks that followed, Olevsky settled into the routine of the Mactavish household. At first, he was cautious about going out, and would only venture forth after he had carefully looked up and down the road to see if there were any unfamiliar cars or any other sign of strangers. It was a quiet corner of Scotland, and there was nothing untoward to be seen. But he remained uneasy and one evening he confessed his concern to Mactavish.

'I fear that they will come after me,' he said. 'They will be wondering where I am. They wait for a few weeks usually – just in case – and then they decide that there has been a defection.'

Mactavish listened. 'You'd think they would leave a poor fellow alone,' he mused.

Olevsky nodded. 'They have long memories,' he said. 'I only hope they don't have any idea of where to look for me.'

'I think you're safe,' said Mactavish. 'And if they come snooping around here, the dogs will let us know. They're great ones for barking at strangers.'

Olevsky smiled. He was growing increasingly fond of the Mactavish family – and of Kirsty in particular – and he did not want anything to imperil that. And yet he knew that the

KGB had a long reach, and that the Scottish Highlands were well within their range. And he was right: a few days after this conversation with Mactavish, as he was making his way into the village to pick up his host's copy of the *Oban Times*, he noticed a man standing near the ferry slipway, innocently smoking a cigarette. Olevsky stopped as the smoke drifted over towards him. It had the unmistakable smell of Russian tobacco.

He looked over his shoulder. The man was watching him, and now he approached him, walking purposively. Olevsky froze. If he ran, then the man would almost certainly fire at him – and he was unarmed. This is how it ends, he thought.

The man came up to him and Olevsky gasped. It was his colleague, Topornin. They had trained together and had spent many happy evenings drinking vodka and telling stories of the old days at naval college.

'So,' said Topornin. 'This is a nice place you've found for yourself, Oleg Vladimirovich. Very nice.'

Olevsky took a deep breath. If one had to die, one might as well die in comity.

'Oh, it's a fine place, Ivan Ivanovich. It's quiet. It's beautiful. The people are friendly.' He paused. 'Would you care to come and meet my new friends?'

Topornin hesitated. Then he said, 'I could do with a spot of lunch.'

'Then come back with me,' said Olevsky. 'I caught some mackerel yesterday. They're very tasty fish.'

'I love fishing,' said Topornin.

'Lots of fish here,' said Olevsky. 'You row out into the bay and come back with ten, twenty fat mackerel.'

'Oh, my goodness,' said Topornin.

They walked back to the farm together. There Olevsky introduced Topornin to Mactavish and to Kirsty. Then they had lunch together. Mactavish gave Topornin a large glass of whisky, that the Russian downed in a single swig.

'All Russians like to drink,' joked Olevsky.

The party continued into the afternoon. At four o'clock the local postman called in with the mail. He and Topornin talked about fishing. More whisky was consumed.

Kirsty's friend, Heather, called in at six. Kirsty played a Russian record that Olevsky had given her. Then Heather and Topornin danced together until they all sat down to dinner.

'Do you think I could find something here too?' Topornin asked Olevsky as they began the venison stew that Kirsty had made.

'Oh, definitely,' said Olevsky. 'But what about ...' He nodded his head in the direction of London – or it could have been Moscow.

Topornin put a finger to his lips. 'They don't know where I was heading,' he said. 'I told them I had a lead, but I didn't give them any details. We're safe here, I think.'

'You're a real friend,' said Olevsky.

'Are there any formalities, though?' Topornin enquired.

'Not here,' said Olevsky. 'You don't have to report to any-body. You just ... get absorbed.'

'Wonderful,' said Topornin.

Olevsky proved to be very handy on the fishing boat. He was also a rather good plasterer, and gradually started doing more of that in houses throughout Lochaber. He and Kirsty married eight months later, and began work on a bunga-low for themselves a few hundred yards from Mactavish's farmhouse, in exactly the spot where the road was to have been built. That plan had been scrapped as the council had experienced a budgetary deficit and had other, more pressing needs to attend to. For Mactavish, that was a victory that gave him immense satisfaction.

Topornin and Heather married a few months after the wedding of Olevsky and Kirsty. They built a house on a plot of land further up the glen and Topornin got a job as a deputy postman. He loved the uniform. Heather was proud of him.

Mactavish had two grandsons over the next four years. Olevsky loved to dress his sons in kilts and shower them with gifts sent over from his aunts in Leningrad. When the Soviet Union fell, these aunts came to Scotland for a holiday and brought even more gifts for the boys. They invited Mactavish to visit them in St Petersburg, which he did with enthusiasm. The aunts told him about the popularity of Robert Burns in Russian translation. 'He speaks to the Russian soul,' they said. 'He really does.'

Olevsky framed a copy of the Corran Ferry timetable and hung it on the wall of their kitchen. People commented on this odd choice of decoration, but he said nothing to divulge the reason behind it. Training in the keeping of secrets often survives a change in one's circumstances.

In the summer, on warm days, he and Kirsty, accompanied by their two sons, would follow a path up to a pool at the bottom of one of the waterfalls. They would swim in the bracing clear water and then, while the boys played at the edge of the pool, the parents would lie back in the heather and look up at the sky, on such days cloudless, a pale blue witness to their happiness.

Donald and Yevgeni

The man with the scholarly air opened the photograph album. He handled it gently, in the way of a porter in an auction house holding an Old Master drawing. He was not wearing the white gloves that such porters wear, but there was in his expression much the same care and reverence.

'These photographs were passed on to me by my grandfather,' he said. 'Long deceased. His entire career was in the consular service. He was an indiscriminate photographer. He snapped everything.'

The woman nodded. 'How useful.'

'Yes. He said to me, you know, that he could not understand how people could do without having a photographic record of their lives. It was beyond him.'

The woman said that she saw how one might feel that. She was not a photographer herself – apart from the occasional family picture – but she enjoyed looking at other people's photographs. 'Although I must confess that sometimes I find them sad.'

'Why should they be sad? Particularly if the people in the photograph are smiling – as they usually are? Why sad?'

She looked thoughtful. 'I find them sad because when the photographs are older ones, I reflect on the fact that everyone in the picture is likely to be no more. It's to do with the transience of life.'

'*Vita brevis est*?'

'Exactly. It is.'

He thought of something. 'In the past, people in photographs kept their mouths closed – for the most part.' He paused. 'And you know why?'

She waited for him to explain.

'Because of their teeth. People used to have gaps. It was very common. Gaps or rotten teeth. Dental hygiene in those days was not what it is today.'

She winced. Anything to do with teeth or nasal passages made her wince.

'I was looking at a photograph the other day,' he went on, 'of a group of soldiers going off to France. Some of them boys, or not far off it. 1914.'

'How sad.'

'Yes, it was. But I don't think they knew what they were in for. They were all very cheerful and smiling. So, we saw their teeth. Most of them, as far as I could see, had lost some. Either that or there were lots of blackened stumps.'

They were silent. He pointed to one of the photographs. It was a black-and-white picture taken in an office somewhere. A man sat at a desk, while another stood behind him. In the corner was a third figure, wearing a strange costume. The man in costume was diminutive.

'See?' he said.

She peered at the photograph.

'Washington,' he said. 'The man sitting down is the British ambassador, a man called Archibald Clark Kerr. A very colourful character, which is putting it mildly. Behind him there, that tall, distinguished-looking man is Donald Maclean. He was at Gresham's School, Norfolk, where I went actually. It's how I became interested in him. Britten was there too. You can see his name on a board in the school hall – and Maclean's, too. A prize of some sort. Then he went on to King's College, Cambridge. He was a member of the Apostles. You know what that means?'

She nodded. She had a vague idea. 'A secret society in Cambridge, wasn't it? John Maynard Keynes – and others.'

'That's them. They met to read one another papers and discuss issues of the day. They were self-consciously elitist. A bit precious. In fact, really precious. Wittgenstein was a member. He didn't like it very much.'

'He wouldn't fit in, I imagine.'

'No, he was odd. He used to sit in a cinema in Cambridge eating buttered toast. I don't know where I read that and whether it's true. It's one of those things that sticks in the mind. Then he wrote the *Tractatus Logico-Philosophicus*.'

'Now, there's a title.'

He smiled at that. Pointing at the standing figure in the photograph he continued, 'Maclean was very urbane, don't you think? First Secretary in the embassy. The consummate British diplomat. And in the corner there – that's Yevgeni Yost, the ambassador's Russian valet, believe it or not, dressed as a Cossack. A dwarf, as they called such people in those days. And still do, I think, although there may be a new term – it's so difficult to keep up.'

She stared at the photograph. 'Are you serious?' she said. 'Do you mean to say that the British ambassador to Washington had a *Russian* valet?'

'He did. Yes. Given to him by Stalin at the end of his posting to Moscow. Archie Clark Kerr was ambassador there before he went to Washington, and got on very well with Stalin.'

'You said: *given?*'

'Yes, that's the sort of thing you could do if you were Stalin. Slavery has had many different faces, remember.' He paused. 'It's all there in accounts of those times. Look it up.'

She searched for words, and decided on, 'Good heavens.'

He looked at her quizzically. 'How many idealists do you see in that photograph? One? Two? Three?' He paused. 'And how many spies?'

She shook her head. 'Who knows?'

'I do,' he said. And then added, 'Although, when I look at this picture I find myself asking, *How many people keep tiny Cossacks in their office?*'

She laughed. 'Is this really true? It isn't some imaginative spy story?'

'Absolutely,' he said. 'Every last word of it. Listen.'

The ambassador first. Archibald Clark Kerr, Lord Inverchapel as he became. He was actually born in Australia, but he always made a great thing about being Scottish, although he never actually lived there. That happens a lot, of course. Some of the most Scottish people there are actually don't live in Scotland. Identities are interesting, aren't they? We can pick the one we feel best expresses something within us. You can be Catholic, or Jewish or have a particular sexual identity or whatever while obviously being something else as well. And you can create an identity for yourself that can then become the real you. Then people think that you were always what you claim to be, that you were born to it, so to speak, rather than having made it all yourself. And that can be important in the world of spies. They are accustomed to maintaining one identity while really being something else altogether.

His father was a Scotsman who emigrated. He married into a well-to-do Australian family – his wife was the daughter of the Premier of New South Wales – but he came back to Britain when his son, Archie, was only seven. So the boy spent the rest of his childhood in the United Kingdom and was not to make much of his Australian heritage. When he eventually made it into *Who's Who*, his entry made no mention of where he was born, nor did it reveal where he went to school, which was in Bath. He was sent to a school there that eventually collapsed – it had its aspirations, but it was never very successful. So, Archie described himself in his *Who's Who* entry as having been 'privately educated'. He also took ten years off his age in that entry, which is an odd thing to do, even in a man who dyed his hair. But then Archie Clark Kerr *was* odd. He would never have made it in the civil service today, let alone in the Foreign Office. But times were different then. There were *characters*, you see, and there wasn't the same expectation of conformity. We think that *they* were stuffy. We think that *we* are free of all that. But the truth of the matter is that we are just as conformist as they were. We delude ourselves if we think we are free – all that has happened is that the nature of the constraints has changed – the diktats are different, and issued by a different set of diktat-issuers. We have a hegemony of attitudes just as they did in the 1920s and 30s. What do they say? *Plus ça change, plus c'est la même chose* ... Except that I think the French never actually say that. We do, and saying it in French adds something, don't you think? A certain *frisson*, perhaps.

The diplomatic service that Archie entered in 1906 was very different from its modern equivalent. Entry was by competitive examination, but was far from open to all. Not everybody could afford to apply: junior staff were expected to have a private income sufficient for the needs of somebody in their position – an important consideration, bearing in mind that they were not paid at all until they had been promoted to the level of third secretary. Once in post, their duties were mundane – opening letters, deciphering telegrams, and filing. Much of their time was spent in idle pursuits of one sort or another, and although they were not as free from duties as were Trollope's non-resident clergymen, the hours were far from demanding. Further up the ladder, Foreign Office mandarins tended not to start their day's work until after eleven in the morning, which left relatively little time to work before they went off for lunch.

Archie's first posting was to Berlin, a place that failed to inspire him, in spite of its diplomatic importance at the time. Like any young diplomat, he was expected to spend a great deal of time mixing in German high society, and he did this with a degree of success. In the summer there was golf and tennis parties; in the evenings there were full-dress balls with dance cards and gossip. There was no shortage of opportunities for flirtations and affairs, useful in making contact with those who knew what was going on in government. Archie was charming, and women liked to confide in him. He soon developed a close friendship with Princess Sophia, the Kaiser's sister, who was married to the Greek crown prince, Constantine. This relationship, in which he played the role of confidant, was typical of the friendships that Archie was capable of establishing amongst the well-placed.

The Greek royal family, into which Sophia had married, was every bit as colourful as Archie himself. Her brother-in-law was Prince Andrew of Greece, a handsome, monocled figure whose disastrous military career culminated in his arrest, trial, and sentencing to death. He was eventually rescued through the intervention of George V, who arranged for him to be taken by gunboat from Corfu, where he had a villa. Included in the party of fleeing royalty was Andrew's son, Philip, who was later to emerge as the Duke of Edinburgh. Andrew's wife eventually became a nun in an order of her own creation, although she still continued to smoke heavily and play canasta. Her good works, though, were numerous, and included the sheltering of Jews during the Second World War. Prince Andrew lived in hotels and villas in the south of France and Monaco until his death in 1944. His family was split by conflicting loyalties during the war years. While Prince Philip served with distinction in the Royal Navy his three sisters, unfortunately, moved in rather different circles, and married German princes of one sort or another.

Archie was to have more involvement with unstable royalty in a subsequent posting, this time at more elevated level, to the British Embassy in Baghdad. Iraq was important to British interests and his posting, as with his time in Cairo, allowed him scope to exercise his intelligence and his sensitive understanding of political trends. The King of Iraq,

King Ghazi, was the son of King Faisal I, the monarch who had been put in place by the British, who controlled Iraq after the dissolution of the Ottoman Empire. Ghazi was educated in England from the age of thirteen and wore western dress. He married and produced an heir, but he also relished the company of the young male servants with whom he surrounded himself. One of these, a favourite to whom he was particularly close, was shot by his own revolver, an incident that was alleged by some to have had something to do with the queen, who took a poor view of her husband's young friends.

Ghazi's behaviour was not approved of by the British authorities. Their spies in the palace reported to Archie on the king's every move and indiscretion. Even he, with his liberal and unconventional attitudes, was surprised by what went on in the palace, which included frequent organised pillow fights between the king and his young male courtiers and servants. The king had picked up an interest in this particular pastime during his boarding school education in England, and never lost his enthusiasm for them. His pillow fights in Baghdad were legendary, and were the subject of ribald comment. In spite of all this, or perhaps because of all this, Archie liked the king, and presumably was upset by his early demise in a highly suspicious car accident – if, indeed, the accident had anything to do with the king's death. One of the five doctors who signed the death certificate confessed decades later that the real cause, in his view, was a blow to the back of the head with an iron bar, suggesting that the accident was a cover-up. The most obvious beneficiaries of the king's death were certain shady commercial figures in Iraq, not that anything was ever proved.

Archie took all this in his stride although his progress up the Foreign Office ladder was not entirely smooth, and there were periods when he felt his career was blighted by official disapproval. He was liberal in his sympathies – the opposite of the stuffed-shirt figures who still influenced British diplomatic thinking at the time. Many of them still harboured imperialist ambitions, believing that they could ride out the enthusiasm for self-determination that now began to challenge the old European empires. In Cairo, Archie understood the feelings of Egyptian nationalists who wanted to overturn the British mandate and pursue the cause of Egyptian independence. British policy, though, was at odds with this current, particularly when it threatened British control of the Sudan. When he appeared to favour policies at odds with London's view, it was not surprising that he should incur official displeasure and consequently be given the impression that his career was stalled.

Although his natural talent and his capacity for hard work was to bring about his rehabilitation – resulting in his appointment to the senior position in the British Embassy in China – this tension between his sympathy for the underdog and the interests of those battling against the odds, was to continue to make it hard for him to implement official policy. This was certainly the case in China, where he had to tread a delicate path between helping the Chinese in the face of Japanese aggression while at the same time avoiding direct involvement in the Sino-Japanese war then in progress. Above all, he needed to avoid Japanese control bringing an end to the British trading concessions in Shanghai and elsewhere in China.

Shanghai, 1939, in the British Residency

He stood before the mirror, adjusting his bow tie. One could buy ties already made up, with wire in the bow to keep them from dropping, but he would never resort to those. He had overheard somebody calling a tie like that a 'cad's tie', which had amused him – not that he was too concerned about how other people dressed. He took care with his own wardrobe, of course, and rather liked dressing up when given the chance. The full diplomatic uniform, with its gold braid, its frogging and its sword, looked good, even if at times it could be unbearably hot. He had donned that when he had presented his credentials to the Kuomintang government, and had been pictured with their officials, clutching his plumed tricorne hat.

Tonight's dinner was not a full-dress affair and so he was wearing a simple dinner jacket and black tie. His two guests, whom everybody was looking forward to meeting, had been told that the invitation was evening dress, and he hoped that they would have managed to find something. They were staying for a few days, and so he could always fix them up if more invitations came their way.

He looked into the mirror at his wife, Tita. She was seated at a dressing table, brushing her hair.

Archie said, 'Somebody said that I looked like Noël Coward when I'm in my dinner jacket. Do you agree?'

She looked in her own mirror, and their eyes met somewhere in the complex optics of the two reflections.

'Noël Coward? Maybe. A bit. He can sing, of course. And play the piano.'

'I said *look* like – not *sound* like.'

'I'm not sure that anybody would want to look like Noël Coward.' She paused. 'And anyway, who are these two? I'm not sure whether I want them to stay.'

He sighed. 'Too late. I've invited them.'

'I wish you'd ask me.'

'They're work.'

She looked doubtful. 'Are they?'

'You know I have to entertain people who turn up. It goes with all this ...' He waved a hand about. 'It goes with the job.'

'But poets? Didn't you say they were poets?'

'One is. The other one is a novelist, and dramatist, I think.'

'Which is which?'

He explained. 'Auden is the poet. His friend is called Isherwood. Auden's the better-known of the two.'

'Where did you pick them up?'

He brushed at his shoulders with a clothes brush. He did not like her choice of phrase. He had not picked these two up, and he was irritated that she should take that approach. After all, he had picked *her* up on a beach in Chile. She had been sitting there and his dog had run across the sand towards her. So if anybody had initiated the picking up, it was the dog. She had been eighteen. He had been forty-seven, a member of the British Embassy staff in Santiago, but he had married her nonetheless. But it was, he supposed, a bit of a pick-up, if one was going to use that term. At least he had made her the wife of the British ambassador to China – and a lady, for that matter. She had rather liked it when he was knighted and she became Lady Kerr.

She looked away. She did not like being in China. She did not enjoy being in Chungking, the seat of Chiang Kai-shek's tottering government, with its mists and its cliffs and its scurrying Chinese officials. She did not like the ever-present threat posed by the Japanese, with their demands and their shelling and their insatiable ambition to devour China and anybody else who threatened their plans for the dominance of Asia. She felt sorry for the Chinese, for the millions who lived in squalor, and for whom distant unconcerned government was the lot to which they had been accustomed for generations. She admired her husband for his stand against the Japanese bullies, even if he had to be careful about what he said. He had to live with a policy of appeasement of the

Japanese invaders and was unable to give the Chinese the aid and support that they needed to combat Tokyo's bullying. He hated that, and she was proud of his distaste for the policy dictated to him by his distant political masters. She admired his courage and the decency that lay at the heart of his dealings with people who were weaker than he was; she admired the way he was able to see the viewpoint of others, particularly of the Chinese, who felt so vulnerable and threatened. She wondered where that came from? The other British people she had encountered since she married him often seemed arrogant and condescending, unquestioning of the privileges that came with birth and the right sort of contacts. Archie was different – he could play those others at their own game; he could affect the same attitudes; utter the right shibboleths; but he could draw on wells of sympathy that they never possessed. Perhaps that was something that came from being born Australian. They said that Australia was an egalitarian society, that it did not matter who your parents were or where you went to school – that what counted was your character, what was inside you. Perhaps that had somehow been instilled in him in those few, early years in Australia, and had never left him. It was quite possible, she thought. And yet she did not want to stay here in China. She wanted to escape the heat and the smells and the emptiness of the diplomatic round. Archie could hardly complain: he worked all the time and when he was not working he liked to sunbathe or paint in watercolours or do anything but spend time talking to her. There was a part of him, she felt, she would never understand, never touch.

'I did not pick them up,' he said icily. 'They were introduced to me. They are here to write about the war.'

She shrugged. 'What's there to say? What have poets got to say about what's going on here?'

'More than you might imagine,' he said. 'I happen to have read some of Auden's work. He's highly regarded.'

She made a face.

'If you read a bit more widely,' he continued, 'then you might know what I mean.'

She threw him a withering glance, before reaching for her lipstick.

He said, 'Why is it that women need to paint their faces? Look at these Chinese women. It's as if they're putting on masks.'

'Perhaps women need masks,' she replied. 'Perhaps men make it necessary for them to have masks.'

They were both silent. He adjusted his bow tie. It was too loose – it was as if it had wilted in the heat. Everything wilted in this heat.

'And who else?' she asked.

'Who else what?'

'Who else is coming to dinner?'

He turned round. 'One or two. Not many. Gunther, if he can make it, which I think he can.'

She sighed. 'Your great friend.'

'Yes, my great friend. One of my many great friends, as you put it.'

Gunther Stein was a journalist. He wrote for everybody, it seemed: *The Christian Science Monitor*, the big English papers, the *Berliner Tageblatt*. He was also a friend of Richard Sorge, a Soviet spy in Tokyo, and had acted as a courier for him.

'Gunther . . .' she mused.

'What about him?'

'Just thinking. I wonder if he likes poetry. Do you think he does?'

'He's a cultivated man. I imagine that he's heard of Auden. They may even have met, for all I know. Auden was in Berlin. And his friend Isherwood was there too.'

She stood up from her dressing table. He was fond of her. He loved having her in the house. *I am incomplete without her*, he thought. *Funny, that. Odd how we need others, and that we are unable to be in the world without somebody at our side. At least, that's what most people feel.* There were always those lone wolves who seemed happy enough with their own company and who did not need the company of others. He was not like that, and he was grateful to her that she had been with him for so long, in all these trying places with all the intrigue and the danger that they encountered there.

Auden and Isherwood were in talkative mood at dinner. When Tita asked Isherwood what he thought of war, he replied, 'War is ghastly. War is sitting around doing nothing, waiting for terror to engulf you. War is not being able to wash or read a book or make love. War is full of dirt and confusion and tears. And it goes on. Day after day after day it's like that.'

She inclined her head. He was right.

She said, 'Did you meet Madame Chiang Kai-shek?'

Auden said yes, they had met her. And she had asked him whether poets ate cake. 'I replied that they did,' said Auden. 'She seemed surprised. She said that she had assumed that they might live on spiritual food.'

'How strange,' said Tita.

From China, Archie's next appointment was that of ambassador to the Soviet Union. This was a crucial posting, particularly when, after Hitler launched Operation Barbarossa, the United Kingdom and the USSR found themselves on the same side in the war. He found the Russians to be difficult allies – suspicious and resentful of the way in which they were treated by the United States and Britain. What the Russians wanted was as much material aid as possible and the opening of a second front that would engage Hitler in the west. There were stumbling blocks in the way of both of these objectives: losses on convoys to Russia were heavy and Churchill and Roosevelt were wary of committing to a firm date for landings in France. It was not easy for Archie to persuade the Russians that their concerns were being addressed and in this way to keep them on board. Fortunately, he got on well with Stalin, who was not always the easiest of company. They shared an interest in pipes and pipe tobacco; it was a rare, and important, friendship.

In the forest

The official dacha stood in a forest clearing. Moscow was not far away, a bumpy ride of barely two hours in any of the diplomatic limousines parked in a circle in front of the dark-green building. Off to one side, a gravelled path led into the trees, its edges marked by stones placed at regular intervals. Only the clearing allowed for light to permeate the arboreal gloom; the city may not have been too distant, but this was the start of another Russia altogether, a Russia of endless, monotonous forests that went on for ever, to frozen tundra somewhere very far off.

Churchill did not like it. He thought of Russia as a gloomy place, with people to match; he felt out of sympathy with their heavy, literal approach, what he thought of as their peasant cunning. He was irritated by Stalin's manner towards him, and at their meeting the previous evening he felt that Stalin had deliberately insulted him. Diplomatically, the meeting between the two leaders was not going well.

Now, walking ahead of Archie, he stamped along the path as it gradually narrowed. As they went further into the depths of the forest, the trees closed in around them, the needles of the spruce scratching their arms, the upper boughs concealing the sky.

'Wretched trees,' said Churchill. 'You'd think they might rise to the occasional oak.'

'Russia,' said Archie. 'There are a lot of these trees.'

'So I have observed,' said Churchill.

Archie focused on the back of the man ahead of him – on the shoulders, slightly hunched when viewed from this angle, and the round head perched on them. Shoulders were a metaphor, of course, for the bearing of a burden – and what burdens this man carried. He and the prime minister had always got on well enough, although in the past he had found himself at odds with Churchill's deeply engrained imperialism. But that, he supposed, was a concomitant of being born on the cusp of great changes: it was understandable that one might suddenly seem out of touch with the world that was emerging about one.

'A very rough figure, our Comrade Stalin,' Churchill suddenly muttered. 'I don't suppose he ever learned any manners.'

Archie found himself addressing the back of the prime minister's neck. People could misjudge Stalin, who was wilier than he might appear – and better educated too.

'You know, of course, that he was training for the Orthodox priesthood. He had a slight change of direction.'

Churchill knew that. 'He claims to have been expelled

from his seminary for revolutionary activities. Do you give that any credence?'

Archie hesitated. '*Cum grano salis.*'

'An embroidering of the truth,' mused Churchill. 'I suppose we all do that to a greater or lesser extent.' He paused. 'Even you, Archie – even you must have occasionally . . . how shall we put it, exaggerated?'

Was this some sort of trap? Archie wondered.

'Me, Prime Minister? You aren't suggesting that I . . .'

Churchill chuckled. 'Everybody has a secret of one sort or another. Diplomats usually have more than one.'

'I assure you, Prime Minister, that what you get with me is what you see.'

'A tall man with a broken nose?'

Archie smarted. Churchill might be prime minister but that did not give him the right to pass comments on one's nose.

When Archie said nothing, Churchill turned round to face him. *You're one to talk*, he thought. *What they say about you having a baby face is absolutely true. All babies look like you, Prime Minister – or you look like all babies: one might take one's pick.*

Archie plucked up his courage. It was not every day that you were called upon to question the prime minister's judgement. He drew a deep breath. 'I think you're being too hard on Stalin.' He wondered whether his voice gave away the anxiety he was feeling.

'Too hard? That man crossed a line. I don't have to put up with it. I represent the United Kingdom. I'm not some Kremlin underling.'

'He doesn't see you as that, Prime Minister.'

Churchill snorted. 'He should choose his words more carefully.'

For a few moments Archie said nothing. Underfoot, the fallen spruce needles crunched against gravel. A bird sang somewhere in the trees – a lonely song that went unanswered.

'You have such great gifts, Prime Minister. You were born with them.'

Churchill slowed down. 'What do you mean by that?'

It was too late to go back. The rebuke, if that was what it was to be, now had to be delivered.

'I mean that God has given you immense talents. You can charm the birds out of the trees. You can hold entire nations in the palm of your hands with your words. You know that, as well as I do.'

Churchill said nothing.

'And I've seen you use that . . . well, one simply has to call it *charm*; I've seen you use that to get people to see things from your point of view. Or to put people at their ease and make them want to help. I've seen it. And yet here you are with this . . . this rough and ready street fighter – for that's what he is, after all – about to get on your high horse and threaten everything in the process.'

'He insulted me.'

Archie raised his voice. It was unintentional, but it made Churchill slow down again, even if he did not turn round. 'But that's what they're all like, Prime Minister. They don't mince their words. They don't know how to. They think aloud. They don't mean to offend; it's just that they don't seem to understand tact, or subtlety, or whatever you like to call it. They're pretty basic, when all is said and done.'

Churchill was listening. Now he snapped, 'He can fight his own battles – if that's the way he wants it.'

Archie caught his breath. This was a moment of profound danger. If Churchill fell out with Stalin, then the Russians might draw the conclusion that they were on their own. And if they thought that, then there was always a possibility that they would try to negotiate their own peace with Germany. It did not take much imagination to envisage the consequences of that: with his eastern flank secure, Hitler would be free to concentrate on the consolidation of his earlier gains in the west. With that, and with Allied exhaustion, the whole course of the war could be changed. He looked up at the sky, or at such of it as was visible through the branches of the trees. The world was so precious, so beautiful – so fragile. Civilization hung by a thread, and had always done so, perhaps, although it was only occasionally that we realised it.

He bit his lip. If the heart within this familiar, obstinate figure before him were to stop, then that great battle, which Churchill himself had identified in his oratory, would be lost.

People would give up. The fight could go out of them. That could happen – it really could. But it was not just on that single beating muscle that everything depended; it depended, too, on what he, Archie, said next. Now it was him upon whom the fulcrum of history rested. Him: Archie Clark Kerr, Australian, Scotsman, Knight Commander of the Order of St Michael and St George, who had wandered into history and now had to do what history demanded of him.

'Prime Minister,' he said, his voice more controlled now. 'Prime Minister, Stalin wants in his own rather clumsy way to patch things up. I saw what happened last night at the dinner. I saw him following you to the door. He wanted to talk. He wanted to say sorry – once again, in his own, unusual way. It would cost you nothing to rise above his social ineptitude. You are a man of standing – you come from a background of distinction and achievement. He comes from nothing. He hasn't had your advantages. You should extend a hand to him. It would make all the difference, believe me.'

Churchill stopped, so suddenly that Archie almost bumped into him. Then he turned round and gazed at the ambassador. 'That's what you think, is it?'

Archie lowered his eyes. 'That's what I think.'

'And I suppose you know what you're talking about.'

Archie raised his eyes again. Churchill was smiling.

'As do you, sir,' said Archie.

Churchill hesitated. 'You could be right,' he said.

'I hope I am.'

Churchill reached into his pocket for a cigar. 'You smoke a pipe, don't you?'

'It's my only failing.'

Churchill laughed. 'Could you get in touch with them? Ask them whether we can have a meeting tonight. Just Stalin and I. No Molotov. Can't stand that fellow and his boot-faced look.'

'He's not known for his humour,' said Archie.

'Fix it up,' said Churchill. 'And lay on some champagne for me so that I don't have to stomach his vodka.'

They turned, and made their way back to the dacha. Archie thought, *I have just been present at a moment which may have decided the fate of western civilization.* His heart gave a lurch. He had always wanted to be at the centre of things – to be in on the making of history. But he had never imagined that it would be like this: a matter of a brief exchange between two men on a path through a Russian forest, with the sky now threatening rain, and the smell of the spruce, that green smell, as he thought of it, mingling with the wisp of cigar smoke from a newly lit cigar; while elsewhere, altogether elsewhere, men fought and died over tracts of land, and flags, and promises that would never be kept. That was nothing new, of course.

Churchill asked him a question that he missed because his mind had been elsewhere.

'I asked,' Churchill repeated, 'whether you think Stalin is well-informed.'

Archie took a few moments to think about his answer. Then he said, 'Sometimes I think he is. Yes. Sometimes I think he knows more than he lets on.'

'Could somebody be telling him things?' asked Churchill. Archie had no answer.

Then Churchill said, 'Could you tell me something amusing about him? About Stalin? Just to amuse me in this God-forsaken place?'

Archie thought for a moment. 'He went to Sweden in 1905,' he said.

Churchill waited. 'And?'

'There was a large party of Bolsheviks and Mensheviks. They were going to a meeting in Stockholm, and Stalin was one of them. They travelled up to Helsinki first to catch a boat across the Baltic. They were an unruly mob, as you can imagine. The Bolsheviks and Mensheviks were always at one another's throats over this, that and the next thing. You know how the Reds love their ideological disputes.'

Churchill grinned. 'Put two cats in a box and they'll fight.'

'Well, they all boarded the boat and discovered that their fellow passengers were an interesting lot. A party of circus clowns, no less, with a whole lot of performing dogs and dancing horses. Quite a passenger list. Anyway, before the ship set off the Bolsheviks and Mensheviks started to argue and a fight broke out. It got worse, and there was a general commotion. The clowns were involved, and, one imagines, the performing dogs. The ship got out of harbour but was shipwrecked a short distance out and everybody had to spend the night on the half-sunk vessel before they were picked up by another boat and taken off to Sweden.'

Churchill reached for a handkerchief and blew his nose loudly. 'My day improves,' he muttered, adding, 'markedly.'

In Cambridge, in 1933

'Very tall,' said Guy Burgess. 'Bourgeois as hell – but aren't we all? Rather good-looking, but then again, aren't we all?' He glanced at the man to whom he was talking. Such a pity. Wrong team: paid-up member of the wrong team.

Kim Philby smiled tolerantly. 'I'm not interested in such things, Guy, dear chap. As you know, I like women. Perverse of me, yes, I admit it. But there have been plenty of us in history, you know. Great artists and composers. Generals and heroes. Possibly even Shakespeare, if you read the *Sonnets* in a particular way. All men who liked women. And women would like you, I believe – if you gave them the chance. And stopped eating so much garlic.'

Burgess waved a careless hand. 'I just don't have the time, Kim. With all these delectable boys about. How could I? And Mrs God, to whom we should all be most grateful, has given me certain talents – I should use those, rather than seeking to diversify.'

Philby looked away. Mrs God! Burgess was deliberately

outrageous. He drank on a reckless scale and boasted constantly, and openly, about his sexual conquests. And yet there was something about him that was strangely compelling. He was vivacious, witty company and seemed to draw people into his orbit with little or no effort. *Charisma* was one word to which resort might be made when talking of Burgess, Philby thought; *simpatico* was another.

And you had to forgive him, all the sex and drink and braggadocio, even the garlic, because his heart was in the right place, and that, ultimately, was what counted. He understood injustice, and its place in human affairs. He understood the theft that had been committed – and that was the only word for it – the theft that had been committed by those who took from the working classes the fruits of their labour. A child should be able to understand that – to see it for what it was – but that fundamental fact, that *ur*-crime, had been so overlaid with cant and edifice that it seemed that only a few could see it for what it was. Yet it was so simple, so *obvious*. Capitalism was simply wrong. It was not complicatedly wrong – it was *simply* wrong.

Look at the whole, rotten edifice, Philby thought. Look at it. The House of Windsor, the Archbishop of Canterbury, the pious platitudes, the police and prisons, the hangman, the servitude of the millions in the colonies, the daily grind of the people who actually made things, who grew the food, who cleaned up, who went down the mines in rattling cages and who died because the coal dust blocked their bronchial tubes. Look at that, and ask your-self how could you possibly not feel complete revulsion. How could you *not*?

But now they were discussing Donald Maclean, who was a fellow undergraduate.

'Tell me about him,' said Philby.

Burgess reached for his martini glass. He had mixed him-self three, and they were lined up to be tackled one after the other. They would not last long. 'What's there to say? His father is an awful Calvinist Scotsman – you know the type.' He fingered the stem of the glass. 'Unbending. A politician. Donald is very different, thank goodness. Sons don't neces-sarily take after their fathers, Kim, which is fortunate for you, because otherwise what would you be? Living in Beirut or somewhere of the sort; probably marrying and having six children by a Nubian girl, my dear – a Nubian! Delicious. Like an apricot, perhaps. All juicy and sweet.'

Philby's father, St John Philby, was a distin-guished Arabist.

'I've never known exactly who the Nubians are,' Burgess continued, draining his martini glass. 'Are they some sort of exotic Egyptian, do you think? Yet another group of people we've taken under our benevolent imperialist fold? I wonder if they write in hieroglyphics? What do you think, Kim? Do you have a theory about that?'

'Don't be absurd, Guy. Or should I say, don't be more absurd than usual.'

128

Burgess embarked on his second martini. 'What does Anthony say?'

'About Maclean?'

'The very same.'

Philby thought for a moment. 'Anthony, as you know, does not waste his words. He's just like that painter of his, Poussin. Cold and classical. Anthony speaks highly of Donald. He thinks he's serious.'

'Which is true, I think. Anthony's right. Donald gives every impression of actually meaning it. You did hear about what he did when he came back for his third year?'

Philby shook his head.

'He sold all his clothes,' Burgess went on. 'The shirt off his back. Everything.' He paused. 'Now, as you know, Kim, I'm all in favour of chaps who are prepared to disrobe ...' The martini was disappearing fast. 'However, in this case, Donald was simply getting rid of his good stuff to kit himself out in second-hand things from those shops that sell clothes to the hard up. Or the poor, as we should not be afraid to call them. Enough of euphemisms.'

Philby raised an eyebrow. 'Rather impressive.'

'Indeed. And he let his fingernails become dirty. Just like mine.' He held up a hand to show Philby. 'Although in my case it's laziness. In his case, I think it's ideological. He said he's planning to live in Russia when he goes down. Seriously. I think he wants to teach English to Russians. Such a noble project.'

Philby shrugged. 'To each his own way of demonstrating solidarity.' He paused. He fixed Burgess with a bemused stare. 'Have you and Donald ... You know ...'

Burgess put down his glass. 'Don't be coy, Kim. But the answer is yes, if you must know. It was a long campaign, though. There are still a lot of defences. His father's fault, of course. John Knox et al. Mind you, he's actually more like you than he is like me, I'm afraid. I don't think he's one of us, or, shall I say, one of me, since you, unfortunately, are so boringly unmusical.' He sighed. 'I don't think there'll be a repeat show. Some plays run only for one night, you know. No encore.'

'I think I shall probably look him up after he leaves Cambridge,' said Philby. 'It's good to keep in touch, I always say.'

'Close touch,' said Burgess, reaching for the second glass. 'The closer the better, in fact. Chin chin, Kim.' He looked at his friend. 'It's rather sweet, I think, how chaps like you can look up people like Donald and never be suspected of ulterior motives.'

'The joy of being of conventional persuasion,' said Philby.

'And wanting only to discuss politics.'

Philby nodded. 'Politics is all there is, Guy.' The levity of the last few minutes disappeared. Now he sounded sombre, even regretful. 'There's a major war coming – sooner rather than later.' He paused, struck by the triteness of what he had just said. How many times had people said that? It had become the most predictable of clichés, in the mouth of the most naïve of undergraduates. How many times did those words occur in newspaper columns, dispensed as if confidential information were being imparted? But that, he told himself, did not detract from the fact that it was true, and needed to be said.

He looked at Burgess. His friend's mask of insouciance had slipped, and he was pleased. Burgess knew when to be serious, even if there were those who thought him incapable of sobering up sufficiently. Philby continued, 'We – you and I – are going to be asked – once again – to die for the established order. Do you propose to go meekly?'

'I don't propose to go at all,' said Burgess. 'Ours is a different battle. And it's already started.' He paused. 'Shall we pour ourselves more drinks? What is happening to these martinis, Kim? *Eheu fugaces, labuntur martini.*'

'Very funny, Guy.'

'Thank you.'

Philby invited Maclean to dinner in his flat.

'Just us,' he said. 'There's a lot to talk about.' He offered his guest a sherry. 'I hope this is dry enough. Berry Brothers. You know their place?'

'I do,' said Maclean. 'I've walked past it. I've never been inside.'

Philby handed him the glass. 'Seen Guy recently?'

Maclean shook his head. 'I've not seen many people. I've been reading a lot. A bit of theatre – not that there's much on at the moment.'

'I saw Guy a couple of weeks ago.'

'Sober?'

'What do you think?'

Maclean smiled. 'When he dies, I hope he donates his liver to medical science.'

Philby gestured for Maclean to sit down. He pointed to his bookshelves. 'Those are all waiting to be read – every one of them. I'll get round to it one of these days.'

'You're working?'

'Yes.'

Maclean waited. Then he said, 'Anything interesting?'

Philby was guarded. 'An international organisation.' He looked at Maclean over the rim of his sherry glass. 'And you? Your plans?'

Maclean replied immediately. 'The Foreign Office. I'm going to do the exams. I'll see.'

'You know I had a little difficulty there,' Philby said. 'My tutor in Cambridge objected to me politically. He said that a radical socialist had no business being a civil servant. His reference put them off. You know what they're like.'

'I'll be careful about my referees,' said Maclean.

'Very wise. With your connections, you shouldn't have too much difficulty getting somebody who'll impress them.'

'Perhaps.'

Philby took another sip of his sherry. 'Do you think you might work for us?'

Maclean looked at him. 'Us being?'

'The cause.'

There was a silence. 'For the Comintern?'

Philby did not take his eyes off him. 'That sort of thing.'

'Yes.'

Philby was taken aback by the speed of the reply. He folded his hands. He seemed bemused. 'That didn't take you long to decide.'

'Why should it?' asked Maclean. 'The lines are clearly drawn, aren't they? I decided some time ago which side I was on.' He paused. 'I'd like to ask you something, though. Will I be working for the Soviet Union or for the cause more generally?'

Philby made a gesture that suggested that the boundaries were vague. 'It very much amounts to the same thing. The one supports the other, and without the Soviet Union, where would communism be? Nowhere? Exactly.'

'I want to,' said Maclean.

Philby put down his glass. 'I was hoping you'd say that.'

'I want to do something useful with my life.'

'You'll get no better chance than this. When I decided, you know, to devote my life to ... to the righting of the great wrong, I felt as if I'd suddenly discovered something that made sense of everything. It was a moment of extraordinary clarity.'

Maclean was staring at the floor. Now he lifted his gaze. 'Like first looking into Chapman's Homer?'

Philby grinned. 'I'm not sure whether Keats quite fits.

But yes, as I said, it was an important moment for me.' He paused. 'It's a commitment, you know. You don't enter upon it lightly.'

Maclean said he knew that. 'I'm serious about it. I've been thinking about it for years. Even at school.'

'And you're sure you're not doing it just to spite your father – or the memory of your father, should I say.'

Maclean blushed. 'I don't think so.'

'I ask that,' said Philby, 'because it's important to know one's motives. People act for very different reasons. Sometimes we're locked in old battles with Nanny, you know. Sometimes with Mother. You've read your Freud, I imagine.'

Maclean became silent, and for a few moments Philby looked concerned. 'I don't mean to belittle your conviction, Donald. I'm acting as *advocatus diaboli* here.'

Maclean nodded. 'I understand.'

Philby looked relieved. 'I think I can arrange for you to see somebody.'

'When?'

'Very soon. In a matter of days.'

'Who is it?'

Philby said, 'He's called Otto. You'll be told by him what he wants you to do. In the meantime, though, this conversation never took place. Speak to nobody about it. Carry on with your plans to do the F.O. exams. Don't advertise your political opinions. Be what you so obviously are.'

'Which is?'

'A typical bourgeois parasite. A privileged member of a privileged caste. None of which would stretch your acting ability excessively, would it?'

They looked at one another. Philby reached out a hand. Maclean shook it.

In Moscow, January 1946

Stalin was pleased with the painting that had been newly hung in his office. His eyes kept moving to it, as if he was willing Archie to make some remark about it. Archie was prepared to oblige, but found that it was taxing his powers of diplomacy to conceal his real reaction. The painting was typical of Soviet Realism, of which school there existed countless examples in the corridors and halls of the Kremlin.

'A very fine painting, this one,' Stalin said. 'That man is a true artist.'

'Yes,' said Archie. He searched for something to say. 'It is a very good likeness of you, I feel. And that's Comrade Voroshilov, I imagine. It certainly looks like him. Remarkably like him – although not as faithful to the original, so to speak, as is his portrayal of yourself.'

'It is indeed,' said Stalin. 'I see that you are an art critic, Ambassador, amongst your many other talents. And, of course, you paint yourself. I have not forgotten that.'

'Amateur daubs,' said Archie. 'Nothing more than that.'

'You are very modest. Unlike Gerasimov, who painted this picture. He likes to remind people that he is a great artist.'

In these latitudes, thought Archie, pride *definitely* comes before a fall.

Archie took out his pipe. He had brought a gift of tobacco with him that Stalin had received enthusiastically and a sample of which he was even now offering his visitor. 'Well, Gerasimov is very popular, isn't he? And justly so, I'd say. There are many people who get pleasure from looking at his paintings.'

Stalin nodded. 'But we are not here to discuss art. We are here to say goodbye.'

'A very sad duty for me, Marshal.'

'We all have to say goodbye sooner or later,' said Stalin. 'It is part of the human condition, is it not?'

'I'm afraid so. There are many things that we do not like, but that are part of who we are.'

Stalin looked sideways at him, seemingly uncertain, for a moment, how to take this. But then he grinned. 'Man can change, though, once the material conditions that determine his nature are changed sufficiently.'

Archie felt that he did not need this elementary lesson in communist theory, but it was his job to be pleasant, and so he simply smiled, inclining his head in an impossible-to-interpret gesture. Stalin never got beyond the level of the predictable, he thought. For all his wiliness, his cunning, there was no moral imagination.

'There is one thing I thought I might raise with you,' Archie continued. 'Since we are parting company.'

'Of course. I was about to ask you if I could do anything to help.'

It was the invitation that Archie hoped would be extended.

'There is a woman who is employed in the embassy. Local staff.'

Stalin watched. *Local staff* was another word for *spy*.

'She is a hard-working woman,' said Archie. 'She has looked after us well.'

'I'm pleased to hear that.'

Archie continued quickly. 'She has a brother.'

Stalin watched him.

'Unfortunately, this brother of hers is in a spot of trouble. He has been accused of desertion. I believe that the army is holding him.'

Stalin shrugged. 'That sort of thing happens in any army – ours included. There are always troublesome elements.'

'I wouldn't doubt that for a moment,' said Archie. 'This man is undoubtedly in the wrong. He deserves to be punished, I'm sure. Severely. But there are extenuating factors in this case. And I wondered whether you might be able to show the mercy that I know you have exercised so generously in so many other deserving cases.'

In diplomacy, thought Archie, you can *never* underestimate the power of flattery, even, or perhaps especially, when it was ill-deserved.

Stalin allowed a smile to cross his face. The eyes, though, were still watchful. 'And what are these factors?' he asked.

'He is a dwarf.'

For a few moments Stalin did not react. Then he laughed. 'Oh, that's very funny,' he said. 'So, the problem's a small one.'

Archie made much of the joke. 'You could certainly say that, Chairman.'

'And you want me to let him off?'

'His sister would be very grateful. She is a good Soviet citizen. She . . .'

Stalin interrupted him. 'A good Soviet citizen with a bad brother?'

'Well, I think he may have been under pressure. They're from the Volga, you see, and recent events, as you can imagine . . .'

Stalin waved a hand airily. 'That's all over now. There's a new world emerging. Those people are not an issue.'

People have never been an issue for you, thought Archie. 'Precisely.'

Stalin thought for a moment. He looked out of the window. Then he turned and said to Archie, 'Why don't you take him as your servant? I am very happy to give him to you.'

Archie gave a start. 'Give him to me?'

'Yes. In the circumstances he's very fortunate, I would have thought. It is quite in order for my government to redirect his labour. He can work for you now. You take him with you. He can be ...' He waved a hand again. 'He can be your house servant. Your valet. You are always very smart, Excellency, and you will need somebody who can iron your trousers and polish your shoes. A very short man will be good at keeping your shoes well-polished.' Stalin laughed. 'Other small jobs like that. He's yours. Give the details to my aides and they will take care of everything.'

Archie was almost too astonished to speak, but he realised that he had just saved a man's life. So he thanked Stalin effusively, and Stalin accepted the thanks as no more than his due. Then they filled their pipes with the new tobacco and Archie told Stalin something about where it was from. 'There's a place called Virginia,' he said.

'And another place called Georgia,' said Stalin, and laughed again.

Dinner in New York

I know it's not ideal,' said Donald Maclean to his wife, Melinda. 'But is there ever anything that's unequivocally right?' He stabbed a spear of asparagus with his fork. 'Is there?'

She looked at him across the table of their restaurant on 52nd Avenue. It was a place she knew well – a French restaurant run by a temperamental Lyonnais; she had been a regular customer, with her parents, before she went to Paris.

It had changed little over the years, and it seemed that the arguments between chef and *patron*, conducted *con brio* in the kitchen but audible in the dining room itself, were very much the same.

'No,' she said in answer to his question. 'Perhaps not. But there are varying degrees of unsuitability, and this arrangement is fairly high on the scale.'

'There's nowhere in Washington,' he said. 'Not just yet. H.E. is going to put in for an increase in my living expenses allowance. Once – if – that gets the nod from London, then we could afford somewhere convenient in Washington. But it's a small town, and there isn't much choice.'

He looked at her fondly. He could not reveal that there was another reason for her staying with her parents in New York while he spent the week in Washington. His controller was in New York and that was where the information was sent from when it went over to Russia. Maclean needed a reason to make weekly trips to New York, and having his wife there provided a pretext that would be above reproach.

'I'm sorry your mother dislikes me,' said Maclean, filling his glass of wine, and then, seeing that her glass was half empty, doing the same for Melinda.

'She doesn't dislike you. I don't know where you got that idea.'

'From her manner. From the way she looks at me. From the way her lip curls.'

'Mother's lip doesn't curl.'

140

Maclean shrugged. 'Would that be because it might give too much away?'

Melinda ignored the barb. So Maclean continued, 'However she does it, she leaves me in no doubt about what she thinks.'

'Of you?'

'Yes, of me.' He stared at her, daring her to contradict what to him had been only too obvious.

Melinda took a sip of her wine. She peered at the menu. 'Snails,' she said. 'There have been world shortages of everything – but never snails. Strange, that.'

She watched him as he refilled his glass. That was almost the whole bottle of white wine gone, and they had not yet even ordered the food. She did not say anything, but his drinking worried her. He was nowhere near as bad as Guy, of course – nobody was – but he was still drinking too heavily. That may have been possible in London, particularly when the bombs were raining down and people were relieved just to be alive, but it was much more obvious here in the United States. Of course, if she broached the subject with him, if she pointed out that his drinking was less acceptable in their new surroundings, then he would simply respond that America was strait-laced and hypocritical and that people didn't drink so much because they simply didn't have the imagination to do that – ridiculous, offensive arguments. She knew that he despised her country; that he thought Americans were dangerous, but the truth of the matter was that it was America that was pulling his exhausted, almost bankrupt country out of its fiscal quagmire, and that if it weren't for America then he wouldn't even have the freedom to express his offensive, bigoted views.

'Has your mother revealed the nature of her objection to me?' Donald asked.

She glanced up at him, and then quickly looked away. Her mother had done that, but she had not intended to say anything to Donald. Her mother found him condescending. She did not like his superior manner. She did not like his teeth. She had said, 'He's typical of a certain sort of Englishman, darling. Not the sort I have too much time for, I'm afraid.'

'You should give him a chance,' she protested. 'You've only known him for two days.'

'Sometimes one can tell these things fairly quickly,' said her mother. 'Immediately, in fact. You develop experience in judging character as you go through life. You can sum things up.'

She felt resentful. 'His teeth are not his fault.' She could have said much more, but she did not want to pick a fight with her mother, who was fighting enough with her father as it was.

Her mother looked at her. 'You say that bad teeth are not one's fault? Is that what you say?'

'Yes.'

'Well, you're wrong, my dear. You're wrong. You've been in Europe too long. You've picked up their thinking about teeth. Or lack of thinking about teeth, I should say. Donald can get his seen to now that he's in America.'

She looked at her mother. She did not understand; she did not even begin to understand Donald, and his complexity, his secret. She could not because she was too convinced of her view of the world and its rightness. There were other visions of the world, though, and Donald had one of them. For her it was all about teeth and smiles and style. Donald hated all of that, and she could understand how he felt. The America of cheerleaders and farm-boys and glib salesmen – that was what Donald disliked so much; more, perhaps, than he disliked the world of British smugness and its concomitant bone-deep assumptions of superiority. He wanted something better for humanity and was prepared to take risks to help those who wanted to bring that about. She admired him for that. She admired him for the love he had for the weak and the voiceless: the people who had been so brutalised in Spain, the multitudes displaced or killed by European fascism, the people who worked in menial, degrading jobs and who would forever be at the bottom of the heap if it weren't for people like Donald who saw their plight and tried to do something about it.

Dinner in Washington

'No snails,' she said. 'Not a snail in sight.'

He took the menu from her and glanced at it before

putting it down on the table. 'This is, in my view, an Italian restaurant with a French name.' He tapped the table. 'Run by Americans.'

'At least they try. Some places don't even pretend to be French.'

He caught the eye of a passing waiter. He tapped his glass. 'Another martini for me please ... and for my wife ...' He looked at Melinda enquiringly.

'*Pour moi aussi*,' Melinda said.

'Excuse me, Mam?'

'Another martini for her too,' said Donald. And then, to Melinda, he said, 'See what I mean?'

They both laughed.

Melinda leaned across the table. 'Tell me about him,' she said. 'I can't wait to meet him, but first I'd like to hear what you think.'

'I've only just met him.'

'But your judgement's always bang on.'

'He arrived yesterday,' said Donald. 'He was in his office from noon. We were all brought in to pay our respects. Not that much was said – and I heard even less.'

She looked puzzled.

'He speaks very quietly.'

She seemed to find that amusing. 'That's not a bad thing, surely. In this town at least. There are enough loud voices.'

'And he's got a very dry sense of humour.'

'Nothing wrong with that.'

Donald looked thoughtful. 'Possibly. Possibly not.'

'What does that mean?'

He chose his words carefully. He knew that she was uncomfortable when he criticised her country. 'It's just that I'm not sure whether you people do irony in quite the same way as the English.'

She pointed out that he had said that the ambassador was a Scotsman. Or even an Australian.

'Paper Scotsman. Australian-born. He lived in England from the age of seven.' Donald paused. 'But the point about irony holds. It can be completely misunderstood on this side of the Atlantic. That's no criticism, by the way – just an observation.'

She bit her tongue. This was to be a relaxed dinner, and if Donald became anxious or morose he would drink even more than usual. She would keep it light.

'Oh well,' she said. 'Tell me about him.'

'He likes to be called Archie,' said Donald. 'And the jury is out – as it always is when there's a new head of mission. They take time to show their hand. However ...' He left the sentence unfinished, and Melinda waited.

He took a sip of his martini, and grimaced. 'Not dirty enough.'

'Archie?'

'He's got off to a flying start.' He grinned. 'He gave a press conference in New York when his ship docked. He didn't take long to raise hackles.'

She asked for details. Lord Halifax, the previous ambassador, had been perfect for the role. Was this new man going to be different?

'Well, the ship he was on was full of GI brides,' said Donald. 'Two thousand, apparently. And all their babies.'

Melinda burst out laughing.

'Yes,' Donald went on. 'All those GIs hadn't hung around over in England. And Archie made a comment about how ugly British babies were.'

Melinda gasped. 'You can't say that,' she exclaimed.

'You can, apparently. And he did. Then he made some remark about baseball, which you *never* do, unless you intend to say how much you like the game and how wrong people are to say it's boring. And he said neither of these things. And finally he referred to the valet he's brought with him.'

'Why would anybody be interested in him?' asked Melinda.

Donald waited for a few moments to give his words greater effect. Then he leaned forward to give his response. 'Because he's a Russian dwarf.'

Melinda's eyes widened.

'And more than that,' Donald continued. 'He told people that Stalin had *given* him to him. *Given*. What he actually said was, *Stalin gave me a slave.*' He paused. 'I gather that nobody could believe their ears. The journalists broke their pencils they were scribbling so fast. Birds fell from the air. The sun stopped in its path.'

'I can't believe it,' said Melinda.

'He has a great sense of humour,' said Donald. 'We'd heard about it, but nobody here imagined it would be wheeled out so quickly – and with such effect. Everybody was left scratching their heads.'

'Well, at least he's not dull,' observed Melinda.

Donald sighed. 'The cousins are at a loss,' he said. He sometimes used the term *cousins* for American counterparts – in an ironical way. 'I had a call today from somebody I know in the FBI and one from a Chicago congressman. The FBI contact asked me whether it was true that there was a Russian with his knees under the table in the British Embassy. I said that I believed the whole man would fit under the table. He was not amused.'

'Have you met him . . . this valet?'

'I saw him,' replied Donald. 'He goes under the name of Yevgeni Yost. He was fussing about Archie. There's no mistaking him – he dresses as a Cossack.'

'This is going to be interesting,' said Melinda.

Donald looked grave. 'I don't like it at all,' he said. 'We don't want any controversy. And none of us knows anything about this man. Who is this Yevgeni Yost? Why did Stalin present him to Archie? Who does he report to?'

'If he reports to anybody,' said Melinda.

'All Russians report to somebody,' said Donald. 'No, this worries me. I know it sounds funny, but it worries me.'

Donald takes work home

Donald was one of the most efficient and hard-working first secretaries in the entire British Diplomatic Service. He had a great talent for condensing complicated documents and explaining them succinctly to the members of the many committees he served. His position papers made complex international negotiations intelligible to participants who might otherwise become hopelessly confused. His advice was always pertinent and time-saving. His superiors were full of praise for an official who did everything asked of him, and whose only flaws were his drinking and tendency to be dismissive of those he considered reactionary or ill-informed. But if he was tactless in some respects; if he could be moody and brooding; if he could show every sign of being haunted by something – regret? – then all of these drawbacks were eclipsed by his competence and sheer intelligence.

And all the while, virtually any important document that came into his possession was scrutinised for possible interest to the Soviet Union, secretly photographed, or at least paraphrased, and then passed on through his Russian handler for transmission to Moscow. Moscow Centre, at the heart of the spiderweb, had a code-name for this most valuable of all agents: Homer. It was through the information that he supplied about British and American intentions that Stalin and Molotov were able to go into every meeting with their western counterparts knowing exactly what the other side's bargaining position was. And importantly, Donald provided regular information on secret aspects of the nuclear weapons programme – at a stage before the Soviet Union had itself built any atomic weaponry.

He regularly took work home in a bulging briefcase that became a symbol for his conscientiousness and habits of hard work. Security was lax, and as First Secretary, and so patently in speech and manner a product of the Establishment, Donald Maclean was above reproach. Yet American suspicions of a significant leak were aroused, and when direct intelligence was obtained from a would-be Soviet defector of there being a high-level spy in the Foreign Office, nothing was done to link these accusations to Donald. The source warned that the spy was Scottish, and that he came from an upper-class background, but before he could reveal anything more substantial, the Russian met a grisly end in a Washington hotel room – a consequence of his impending defection's having been notified to Philby, who was then able to warn the Russians of what was about to happen.

But there were others who were suspicious, and one of these was Archie's Russian valet, Yevgeni. He did not like Donald Maclean, and Donald Maclean did not like him. In fact, Donald had tried, as tactfully as possible, to alert Archie to the consequences of having a Russian valet but had met with amused incredulity.

'I wouldn't make too much of it myself,' he said to Archie. 'But I thought I might mention that I've heard one or two whispering in the State Department about our internal arrangements here.'

Archie frowned. 'Our internal arrangements? What do they mean?'

'Staffing matters,' said Donald.

'None of their business,' snapped Archie.

Donald hesitated. But he knew that Archie liked transparency and would not object to direct speaking.

'Actually, it's about your valet.'

Archie fixed a disingenuous gaze on Donald. 'Yevgeni? How could anybody object to poor wee Yost?'

Donald smiled. 'But they do, I'm afraid. They weren't expecting you to bring a Russian servant. You know what they're like, these people. Positively xenophobic, some of them. It's the Dayton, Ohio view of the world.'

'I still don't think it's any of their business who I have to iron my shirts.'

Donald said that he thought it was wider than that. 'Security. They think he may see things he shouldn't see.'

Archie shook his head. 'Yevgeni would never do that sort of thing. I saved his life, you know. He remembers that.'

'But these people can be put under pressure. Stalin will do anything. He could take Yost's family hostage in order to get him to co-operate.'

Archie remained unconvinced. 'I saved his life, you know. I don't mention that to anybody – normally – but since you bring the whole thing up, I should perhaps draw your attention to that fact. He would no more steal secrets from me than fly to the moon. He knows what loyalty means.' He paused. 'In fact, Donald, I trust him as much as I trust you.'

Donald looked away. He was not enjoying this. 'I thought I should just tell you what I heard. That's all.'

'Well, you've told me – and thank you for speaking about it. But I'll be damned if I'll change my valet just because somebody from Hicksville, Ohio, happens to object to my man being a Russian. And actually, he's a Volga German. They've been in Russia since the eighteenth century, and to all intents and purposes they're Russian, but that's what he is. People have not been very nice to them recently, and I'm not going to add to everything the poor man's been through. He was almost put in front of a firing squad, for heaven's sake.'

Donald said no more. There was a trade meeting coming up and he had to brief Archie about that. So he simply said, 'I thought I'd mention it. It's nothing much.'

'Well, you've mentioned it,' said Archie. 'Now what about this wretched trade fair in Pittsburgh?'

He began to see the valet in places where he had no business to be within the embassy. At first, he thought that Yevgeni was simply trying to find his way around the building and had lost his way in the corridors, but then he began to find him talking to the young women in the typing pool, or making coffee for himself in the kitchen normally reserved for senior staff, or down in the basement, going through boxes of gardening tools left there by the gardeners. He also found him in the embassy library, running his fingers along the spines of the books. Donald was polite, but became increasingly irritated by the apparent ubiquity of this man who, although allowed to be in the building to attend to the ambassador's needs as a sort of constantly-on-duty servant, had no reason to wander into meeting rooms or, even more, into the offices in which correspondence was logged or decoding took place.

Donald raised it with one of the ministers, whom he suspected shared his irritation.

'I know that Archie thinks he's not a security risk,' he said, 'but that man seems to be everywhere – and I mean everywhere.'

'I came across him under a table,' said the minister. '*Under a table.* Can you believe it?'

Donald rolled his eyes. 'I can, actually. What was his explanation?'

'He said that he was looking for something he had dropped.'

The minister snorted. 'A likely story.' He paused. 'This can't go on. I'll have to take this up with Archie myself. But he seems to have a bit of a blind spot when it comes to Yevgeni. He's tickled by the idea of having such an unlikely valet. It amuses him to see everybody's reaction.'

'Perhaps we're going about it the wrong way,' said Donald. 'Perhaps it would be more effective for us to ignore him. If people were indifferent to him, the Boss might agree to get rid of him.'

'We could try, I suppose.'

They did, but it had no effect. And so further representations were made, the volume of complaints from within and without became steadily larger. Archie seemed impervious to the growing feeling against Yevgeni. 'Yost is a simple valet,' he insisted. 'He's harmless. How many times have I told you people that?'

'Many,' said Donald. He was aware he was pressing the boundaries.

Archie threw him a disapproving glance. His tone, which could often be modest to the point of diffidence, now became more authoritative. 'Well, I'm telling you again. Subject closed.'

A summer afternoon in Washington

Washington in August: the slow-moving traffic; the sky liquid with humidity; the torpor of a time of year when the working population was at its lowest; the politicians away; the civil servants unresponsive; the courts empty of litigants; the bands playing slow tunes requiring minimum effort; in such conditions Donald was watching the slow movement of the clock's hands. He came off duty at five and would go straight to the swimming pool to cool off, but there were two and a half hours to go before he could do that. Lunch had been a limp and wilting sandwich and a cold beer. Dinner would be a lonely affair, as Melinda was in New York. He might end up in a bar somewhere afterwards, just for the benefit of the cool air, and then there would be a night of fitful sleep and uncomfortable dreams.

He was not in a mood to encounter Yevgeni Yost in an unoccupied office, but the valet was there, dressed in what Donald presumed was his summer version of his Cossack's outfit – a white linen blouse and baggy, off-white trousers.

'What are you doing here?' Donald snapped.

Yevgeni looked up. 'I am tidying.'

Donald frowned. 'Tidying what?'

Yevgeny shrugged. 'Lord Inverchapel wants a box.' He used Archie's full title – the title he had been given before his arrival in post.

'Why do you think there's a box in this office?'

The dwarf smiled. 'There is always a box in an office.'

'What a ridiculous thing to say,' snapped Donald.

'It is not ridiculous. You are ridiculous. You are very ridiculous.'

Donald had not expected this. He rarely spoke to Yevgeni, and their conversation had previously been limited to mundane, passing remarks. Now something within Donald gave way. 'Get out of here,' he said. 'Stay in the Residency. Just get out.'

Yevgeni's eyes narrowed. There was a light in them, a

hard, sharp light. 'I know who you are,' he said, his voice low. 'I can smell NKVD. I can smell it. You don't think I can, but I can.'

Donald froze. 'You can what?'

'I said: I can smell NKVD, Mr Maclean. And you are it.'

Donald decided to laugh. 'Are you accusing me of something? You? You're daring to accuse me of . . .'

'Of spy,' Yevgeni interrupted, losing, briefly, his grip of English grammar. 'You of spy. Yes.'

'Get out,' said Donald.

Yevgeni took a step towards him. Donald noticed his shoes, which were black and white two-tone. Co-respondents' shoes, as they were known. They were very small – perhaps designed for a woman's foot, he thought.

'They will catch you one day and kill you,' said Yevgeni. 'The police in London. They will catch you.'

Donald turned round and began to walk out. He stopped. He turned round again. 'You call me a spy?' he shouted. 'You? If there's a spy round here, it's you. You are a Russian. Remember that.' Then he said, 'Nobody will believe anything you say. You know that, don't you?'

Yevgeni was staring at him. 'I know that,' he said. 'That is why I cannot say it. I cannot say it because you are Mr Maclean and I am just Yost. I am nobody. Just Yost. And nobody will believe Yost.'

There was silence. Outside somewhere, a car sounded its horn.

'Yost,' repeated Yevgeni.

Donald took a deep breath. There was no danger, or at least there was no new danger here, because this was nothing but a sudden outburst from a ridiculous little nobody. It meant nothing – nothing at all.

In Scotland

Archie eventually gave way. Yost was told that he could no longer serve as the ambassador's valet and would, instead, be employed by Archie on his farm in Scotland. This role he accepted, as he accepted everything that happened to him after that fateful day on which he had deserted from the Red Army. Archie had saved his life, and he was loyal. Unlikely lives can become intertwined.

When, after a relatively short period in office in Washington, Archie returned to Britain, he spent much of his time in Scotland, where he had acquired an estate in Argyll. Yevgeni's role now included not only managing this estate, but also acting as driver to Archie and his wife. They had brought back with them a green Pontiac station wagon in which they would travel from Argyll to Glasgow, with the diminutive Russian at the wheel.

When Donald was identified as the Soviet agent Homer, the blow to Archie was visceral. Whatever criticism may be levelled against his style of diplomacy, whatever may be said of his colourful foibles, he had been a conscientious servant of his country's interest. It was for him a matter of almost unbearable shame that he had unwittingly nurtured in his embassy one of the most influential spies of the twentieth century.

Donald narrowly escaped arrest. He was spirited away to Moscow, where he spent the rest of his life leading a life of exile, along with Philby and Burgess. Burgess drank himself to death; Philby went off with Melinda after she had moved to Moscow to be with Donald. There is more than one form of betrayal. Blunt remained in London, promised immunity from prosecution. He directed the Courtauld Institute, devoting himself to the study of the neo-classical artist, Nicolas Poussin. He expressed bitter regret for his involvement in espionage.

Yost disappeared into obscurity in a remote part of Scotland. Green hills; sea lochs; weather: all these can enfold and erase the past. He thought of Donald Maclean from time to time, and shook his head.

One afternoon, Yost parked the green Pontiac station wagon outside a café in the small coastal town of Dunoon. People travelled down the Clyde from Glasgow to have lunch in this café, before getting back on the boat that would take them home. Yost went inside and ordered himself a meal of pie and chips – typical Scottish café fare. There were a few people in the café, but he recognised nobody.

Sitting at his table, waiting for his pie to be warmed up,

he noticed that there was a man at a neighbouring table who was staring at him. Because of his diminutive size, Yost was used to the stares of others, although usually they would look away if he returned their gaze. This man did not.

The man broke the silence. 'I reckon you have a pretty interesting story,' he said, and smiled.

There was something about the man's directness that appealed to Yost.

'Yes,' he said. 'I have had a very strange life. If I told you about it, you wouldn't believe me.'

The man laughed. 'Try me,' he said.

Yost told him. When he finished, the man sat motionless. 'Is that true?' he asked. 'Are you making this up?'

'Why would I?' asked Yost.

The man looked thoughtful. 'You knew?' he asked. 'You knew it was Maclean?'

Yost nodded. 'Yes, I did. But they didn't look. They refused to believe that somebody like him could be a traitor. They looked at me, and what did they see? I was a far more likely suspect.'

'And do you feel bitter?' asked the man.

Yost looked out of the window. Did he? He was not sure.

'I feel angry for Sir Archie,' he said at last. 'Maclean betrayed his trust. Sir Archie is a good man. He showed me nothing but kindness.'

'I understand,' said the man.

'And kindness is so important,' said Yost.

'Yes,' said the man. 'It is. Maybe even the most important thing.'

Yost's pie and chips arrived. He smiled at the man to whom he had been talking. 'I must have my lunch now,' he said.

The man nodded.

After finishing his meal, Yost said goodbye to the man in the café. He went outside, got into the green Pontiac station wagon, and drove off. Into history.

Each of us has a little bit of history – not much perhaps – into which we can drive off.

Filioque

The invitation was completely unexpected. It arrived in a typed, formal letter, addressed to Pierre Citroën at the French Pontifical College on the via Santa Chiara, tucked away in his pigeon-hole between a note from his philosophy tutor at the Gregorian and an unsolicited leaflet advertising the merits of *Salvatore's Pizzeria di Napoli.* This was a cheap pizzeria, just round the corner, and popular with students at the college. *Why waste your hard-earned money on expensive ambience,* the leaflet proclaimed, *when you can get Rome's best pizzas in a friendly meeting-place right on your doorstep? Ten per cent reduction for seminarians; cardinals, and above, eat free!*

That cheeky offer went down well with the students.

'You'd never see a cardinal in that place,' said Pierre's friend, Alain. 'Not even a bishop. They like those places where it's all starched linen tablecloths and a fancy wine list.'

Pierre agreed. 'Well, *chacun à son goût.* We'll probably end up like them in due course.'

Alain looked doubtful. 'Not me. I've never really seen the point of expensive meals. Food is food, however you cook it. Once you've swallowed it, what's the difference? And what's so special about a linen napkin? Don't paper ones do exactly the same thing? Wipe the same lips?'

Pierre thought about this. His friend was right: the sensation of taste was a passing one. Rich or exotic food might please the palate for a few seconds and then, once chewed and swallowed, it was no different from unbuttered bread or plain potato: the feeling of fullness it provided was indistinguishable. And was it worth paying large amounts for the purely transitory pleasure of sitting in an expensive restaurant, fussed over by attentive waiters? He thought not. There were far better ways of spending one's money: on books, for example, or on good shoes, or on a tube of sandalwood *sapone da barba*, guaranteed to give one a closer and more comfortable shave. The Italians were so good at that sort of thing, Pierre had discovered: they made the best shaving creams and the most invigorating mentholated pre-shaving balms. And the very best coffee, of course. And so many other things that a French seminarian should not be bothering about but that he could not really help himself thinking about from time to time. After all, these things were put on this earth for the enjoyment of mankind and were only sinful if they were given undue weight, which he was far from doing. For he was quite able to take them or leave them, he reminded himself: he had given up coffee for Lent once, and had found it only a slight sacrifice, especially as he had allowed himself to continue drinking tea. There was no essential merit in punishing the flesh, he felt – that had long since been abandoned even by zealots. St Simeon Stylites may have lived on top of a small pillar for more than thirty years, but there would be few, if any, prepared to do that today. Of course, he had read of a contemporary stylite, a Georgian monk, who had lived for years on top of a pillar. In his case, the pillar was a massive outcrop of rock, large enough to allow for the construction of living quarters surrounded by a small curtilage from which to view the world below.

How different that was from his neat, well-heated bedroom in the Pontifical College, with its bookcase, leather-bound easy chair, and mahogany wardrobe. He was not sure whether it would be easier to get close to God on top of a Georgian pillar, at one with circling birds, on terms with the clouds; as it was, his earth-bound bedroom did not preclude the feeling that he often had of being in touch with something greater than himself, something beyond the noisy world of men, something that, in his view, could only be God, or Spirit, perhaps, if you were one of the many these days to whom it did not come easily to use the name of the Deity. And there it was, he thought wryly: that very reluctance manifesting itself, insidiously, in himself.

Now, as he made his way back to his room after breakfast in the refectory, he looked at the envelope he had picked up from his pigeonhole in the post room. He had always been one of those people who liked to examine a letter from the outside before he opened it. Correspondence, he thought, could reveal itself well before it was opened: the postmark, if legible, could tell you where and when the item was posted; if handwritten, the writing on the envelope could speak volumes as to the temperament of the sender; the envelope itself, cheap or inexpensive, heavy or flimsy, would also speak to the importance of the letter it contained. There was no shortage of clues if you looked for them – and more, of course, might be detected if you held the envelope up to the light, as some people did, fearful, perhaps, that a bill or a final demand lurked within.

The letter had been posted locally. The envelope was firm and obviously expensive; his name and address had been typed, in a tall, rather elegant font, and the name of the college was written out in full. His first thought was that it was from the university, but then he realised it would never use such good stationery, its infrequent communications usually being dispatched in cheap brown envelopes or electronically. He was intrigued, but he decided to wait to open it until he was back in his room. Once there, he sat in his leather armchair and used a blunt table knife to open the envelope.

The first thing he noticed was the cardinal's crest at the head of the writing paper. This was not just printed, but was embossed. Below it a typed letter was topped with the handwritten salutation: *My dear M. Citroën*. He read on: 'Please forgive me for writing to you out of the blue. You may recall our meeting last week, brief though it was, when you attended the lecture I gave at the Gregorian. You asked me a very pertinent question and I replied that the issue that you raised was indeed an interesting one and would require some reflection on my part. I have now given your question that thought and would be delighted to give you a few observations on the matter if you would care to meet me for lunch some time next week. If you contact my secretary, Father James Heaney, OSB, at the number above, he will endeavour to find a day that suits both you and me. Until then, I remain, Your servant in Christ, Tommaso di Montalfino.'

He stared at the letter, reading it again, and then again after that. This was the first letter he had ever received from a cardinal, and he found it hard to believe it was intended for him. Yet he remembered the lecture, which had been on a subject in which he had a particular interest – the *filioque* controversy. And he had asked a question, emboldened to do so because nobody else in the audience had seemed willing to do so. And yes, the cardinal had answered him courteously, asking for more time to consider his response. He had expected it to end there, but it had not, and somehow the cardinal had found out who he was, where he lived and was proposing to give him the answer to his question over lunch.

He left his room. Alain's room was a few doors down the corridor, and he made his way there, to find his friend just about to leave for the first lecture of the day.

'Guess who had a letter from a cardinal today?' said Pierre.

164

'That question suggests its own answer,' said Alain, tucking a pen into his pocket. 'And I assume that it's you.'

Pierre nodded. 'Right first time.'

'Be careful,' said Alain, reaching for the linen satchel in which he carried his lecture notes. 'If a cardinal writes to a seminarian, I'd say there's an agenda.'

'I wasn't born yesterday,' said Pierre. He was twenty-three.

His friend's remark had taken the gloss off Pierre's pleasure, and his disappointment showed.

'I'm sorry,' said Alain. 'I didn't mean to sound sceptical. It's just that ...' He shrugged.

'He said that he was going to reply to that question I asked at the lecture. That's all.'

Alain nodded. 'That's sounds innocent enough. And, yes, I'm excited for you, Pierre. Perhaps he's going to offer you a job. Who knows?'

They were both due to graduate in three months and were thinking of their futures. A letter from a cardinal in such circumstances was promising, to say the least.

'Mention me,' said Alain, with a smile. 'I need a job too. And I'm not sure that I want to end up in some dreary parish somewhere.'

'I'll put in a word,' said Pierre, laughing, and added, 'if I get the chance.'

He was not at all sure how such a chance might present itself. One could hardly say to somebody like a cardinal, 'Oh, by the way, I have a friend ...' and then proceed barefacedly to make some request on that friend's behalf. You would have to be more subtle than that – but how? And how should you make known your own needs? Perhaps it would be enough simply to say that you had not yet decided what to do, and that consequently you were open to offers. Such an approach might then be followed with a careless 'Something is bound to turn up', which, if all went well, might lead to a few moments of silence while possibilities of help were assessed.

Or there could be long silences that went nowhere. Pierre and two fellow seminarians had had such a lunch in their first year in Rome, having been invited by a monsignor friend of their bishop to join him for lunch in another pontifical college. After their opening conversational gambits had fallen flat, nobody could think of much to say, and the meal had been consumed in complete silence. He was two years older now, and more confident, but he still felt daunted by the sheer scale of this invitation. This was to be lunch with a *cardinal*, with one who might just as easily be lunching with the Pope himself; and it had all come about because he had happened to ask a question about a theological issue on which he had, by chance, chosen to write his university dissertation. It was all most unlikely – but that, he had come to understand, was how our personal die was cast. A chance remark, an unplanned meeting, might govern the whole course of one's life. People kept pointing that out, and although he could not think of any such incident in his own life, he knew that he might identify one in retrospect. Shape and pattern in our affairs, people said, were often best understood when we looked back at what has happened rather than when we looked forward.

Later that day he contacted Father James Heaney, OSB, as the cardinal's letter had suggested.

'Ah yes,' said the Benedictine. 'His Eminence mentioned that you might be getting in touch. How's your diary looking?'

Pierre caught his breath. He did not have a diary – his life was too regular and unexciting to merit the keeping of a diary, the pages of which would have been largely virginal, apart from the dates of term, which he knew anyway, and the birthdays of his close family, which he was unlikely to forget.

'My diary?' he said.

'Yes,' said Father Heaney. 'We need to find a day on which both you and His Eminence will be free.' He paused. 'We've got a lot of committees in the earlier part of next week, and those meetings have a tendency to go on a bit, but things are looking a bit brighter on Thursday and Friday.'

Pierre thought: *I have no meetings at all – not a single one.* And he might have confessed that, but instead he said, 'Let me look.'

'What about Friday?' asked Father Heaney. 'How does Friday look to you?'

'That would suit me very well,' said Pierre. He felt ashamed of himself: he should not have pretended in this way. He should have said, right at the outset, 'Look, Father Heaney, I don't even have a diary – let alone anything to put in it.' That's what he should have done, and yet he had not.

'Well, that's grand then,' said the secretary. 'Any dietary preferences?'

Again, the question took Pierre by surprise. Nobody ever bothered to ask him whether he could eat anything – the food was simply placed in front of him and he ate it. He was not particularly fond of root vegetables, but he could eat them, and he did not like anchovies, but once again he could eat them if pressed. So now he simply said, 'I'm not fussy.'

This seemed to please Father Heaney. 'That's a refreshing change,' he said. 'The number of people these days who give you a long list of their likes and dislikes – it happens virtually every time. I was talking the other day, you know, to an archbishop – and I shan't name him, if you don't mind – who seemed to be able to stomach only lettuce and feta cheese. Quite frankly, I'm surprised he's still with us, but there we are.'

They moved on to the location. 'His Eminence is particularly fond of a small restaurant called *La Regola*,' Father Heaney went on. 'You may be familiar with the area. It's off the Campo de' Fiori. In fact, you may know the restaurant itself. It has quite the reputation.'

Pierre knew no restaurants at all – apart from *Salvatore's Pizzeria di Napoli* – and so he replied, 'I don't think I do.'

'Well, it's really very good. I had lunch there last week

with some Brazilians. They loved it. Fortunately, they were paying . . .' The Benedictine laughed, and Pierre thought: *I assume the cardinal will pay,* but what if he said, 'Let's go Dutch?' No, that was impossible.

They arranged the time, and then Father Heaney steered the conversation towards its close. 'A final thought,' he said. 'Before you ring off, tell me: when do you graduate?'

Pierre told him. But, even as he did so, he asked himself what had prompted Father Heaney's question. He had hardly dared hope that they were thinking of offering him a job, but why else would they have wanted to know about his graduation date?

'I see,' said the secretary, and then, 'Well, His Eminence will look forward to seeing you on Friday.'

The conversation concluded, Pierre went to the window of his room and gazed out onto the street below. He felt that something had changed. He was not sure what it was, but a few minutes ago he had been unwilling to think about his future after graduation. Unlike Alain, he had not been contemplating becoming a priest, imagining that he would end up as a teacher of some sort, or a scholar, if he were lucky. A university post would suit him very well, he thought – something in a department of theology, perhaps, where he could think about issues of the soul and spirituality without having to pretend to have the answers. Such thoughts as he had entertained about the future were vague: now it seemed to him that something concrete might present itself. Many of the cardinals exercised extensive patronage, being able to nominate candidates for doctoral research programmes or fellowships. Something of that sort might now be in the offing, and the prospect was frankly exciting. Even if he would eventually return to France, he would be more than happy to stay in Rome, which he found more interesting than his native Bordeaux. He spoke fluent Italian now; he knew his way about the city; he had a good circle of friends.

He left his room and made his way downstairs, out into Rome, into the city in which centuries of history had seeped into the very stone that made the bustling streets, the alleyways, the silent courtyards. He looked up at the windows behind which the people of Rome lived their lives. This was a city of mystery and intrigues, and this mystery into which he was being enticed – this unusual invitation – was one that he now awaited with considerable anticipation. But Friday was a few days off, and he would have to stop thinking about it and concentrate on his work. He had an essay to write for his theology tutor, a critique of Karl Barth's rejection of natural theology. His tutor, a Jesuit, prided himself on his ecumenical openness to Protestant thinking, although, when pushed as to the issue of ultimate truth, he always smiled a wan smile before announcing, 'Such a pity that they're all wrong.'

On Friday he left for *La Regola* well in advance of the time agreed with Father Heaney, killing time by lingering for fifteen minutes in a nearby bookshop. In the restaurant, the proprietor greeted him with surprising deference. He seemed to know whose guest he was, muttering, 'Of course, of course,' as he showed him to a table in the window.

'This is where His Eminence always sits,' the proprietor said. 'It gives a view of what is happening in the street.'

This observation was delivered with a knowing look, and with the addition of, 'Important, that.'

Pierre was uncertain what to say, and so he simply nodded. He sat down, and within a couple of minutes a waiter returned with a bottle of chilled sparkling water. Pierre began his wait, paging through a copy of *Corriere della Sera* that a previous diner had left on a nearby chair. He found it difficult to concentrate on the newspaper, though, which was full of reports on internecine Italian political feuds and dire warnings of impending economic crisis. The government, the paper announced, would more or less certainly fall, possibly by the end of the following week. In France, there were riots pencilled in for next Tuesday, and, if the weather was favourable, for the succeeding two days. There would be a possible meteor strike the week after that. He sighed. The affairs of men were far from simple. The Peaceable Kingdom, the dream of poets and artists, was simply that – a dream.

And then, almost without Pierre noticing his arrival, the cardinal was there, ushered to the table by an obsequious waiter.

Pierre rose to his feet. Unhesitating, as if prompted by ancient custom, he took the proffered hand, bowed slightly, and kissed the band of gold on the cardinal's ring finger.

Tomasso di Montalfino was a tall, well-built man in his fifties, which was young to be a member of the College of Cardinals. His features were aquiline, his eyes suggesting an acute, appraising intelligence. A slight fleshiness provided the only hint of the aura of good living about him. His voice, as he greeted Pierre in Italian, was quiet and controlled. This was a man who spoke succinctly and who normally had no need to repeat himself.

'I am glad you could fit me in,' he said as he sat down.

Pierre showed his surprise. 'But, Your Eminence, it is you who must be busy.'

The cardinal smiled. 'I have my busy times,' he said. 'But then again, there are occasions when time hangs heavy.' He nodded to the waiter, who went off obediently towards the kitchen. Fixing Pierre with an inquisitive stare, he asked, 'Your name – Citroën ... I'm sure everybody must ask you the same question.'

'They do,' said Pierre, adding hurriedly, 'but I don't mind.'

'I owned a Citroën once,' said the cardinal. 'A Traction. A lovely car. It was probably the best car I shall ever own.' He paused. 'I take it there's a connection?'

Pierre felt a stab of disappointment. So this was it: the cardinal had assumed that he was a member of the car-manufacturing dynasty. That would explain the invitation: cardinals were not above simple snobbery.

'I'm sorry to say,' Pierre began, 'but we're a different branch. In fact, I believe we have nothing at all to do with the car people. We know about them, of course, and there may be some ancient connection – way back – but we're really a different family. I think we all have a Netherlands connection, but it's pretty obscure. We all go back to some early lemon-growers – hence the name.'

The cardinal did not seem disappointed. 'Ultimately,' he said, 'we're all cousins anyway, aren't we? Isn't that what the population geneticists tell us? That all of us here in Western Europe are descended from a handful of women?'

'I've heard that,' said Pierre.

'And that's rather reassuring, don't you think?' said the cardinal. 'The idea of universal brotherhood is being borne out by science. It provides additional authority, I think, for the brotherhood we've been talking about all along.'

'And for *agape*,' said Pierre.

'Yes,' said the cardinal. 'And for *agape* too. Is it easier to love those to whom you know you are somehow related, even if rather distantly? I think that possibly it is.'

'Perhaps,' said Pierre.

The cardinal sat back in his seat. 'Of course, the requirement to love others,' he said, 'is at the heart of our Christian message, isn't it? And if we hadn't had that underpinning our civilization, I wonder whether we would necessarily have gone down the route that we have tried to go down for the last couple of thousand years. It could have been quite different, you know.' He paused. 'Sometimes I wonder where contemporary proponents of human rights think their values came from. They can be very dismissive of us – of the Christian tradition – but has it occurred to them that the values they are so attached to are a direct result of Christianity's stressing of dignity and love? I think perhaps not.'

'Yes,' said Pierre, and then added, 'Or should I say no. I suspect they don't think of it that way.'

'Then their sense of history must be rather defective,' said the cardinal. 'Mind you, I am never in the slightest bit surprised by ignorance. Look at contemporary fascists. Do they know what happened in the 1930s? I don't think they do. Or some of them don't – hence their willingness to peddle the political poison they espouse.'

'No.'

'And do people remember what Stalin did? Do they remember the Terror? Do they know how many millions died at the whim of a single paranoid dictator?'

'I think they might not,' said Pierre.

The cardinal fixed him with an unnerving gaze. 'But you do? Am I correct?'

'I don't know much about Russian history, but I do know about some of it.'

For a few moments, the cardinal seemed to toy with the idea of taking the point further, but then he said, 'Tell me a bit about your family – your Citroëns.'

'I think we were Dutch,' said Pierre. 'I had an uncle who loved doing family trees. He traced us back to the beginning of the nineteenth century, but didn't come up with anything earlier than that. We went to France in the 1860s. To Clermont-Ferrand, initially.'

'And?'

'And set up a shoe factory,' said Pierre. 'That lasted until the early 1930s. We made boots for the army, including the Foreign Legion. The factory did well.'

'I can imagine that,' said the cardinal.

'My great-grandfather lost interest in the shoe business,' Pierre went on. 'He left Clermont-Ferrand and went off to Bordeaux. He became a *négociant* in the wine trade. That is what the family has done since then. My father still runs the business.'

'A pity about the shoes,' said the cardinal. 'Shoes are so interesting. Have you ever come across Belgian shoes?'

Pierre shook his head. 'Not as far as I know. I don't ask where my shoes are made. They're not expensive, of course.' He paused. 'Is there something special about Belgian shoes, Your Eminence?'

'They are very comfortable,' said the cardinal. 'They're what the Americans call loafers. They're very light and you only wear them inside – unless you have special soles put on them. The original soles are compressed horse-hair covered with soft leather. That makes them remarkably light.'

Pierre glanced under the table; he could not stop himself. The cardinal smiled. 'I'm not wearing them now,' he said. 'But I like to wear them in my study. They aid concentration, for some reason. Perhaps it's because you cease to be aware of your feet. If you don't have to think about your feet, then you can think about higher things, so to speak.'

The waiter arrived to take their order. He approached the table very slowly, almost tentatively, but was encouraged by the cardinal. 'We're ready, Enrico,' he said. 'Or I am and I'm sure my guest will make up his mind quickly enough. Remind us of today's specials, if you please.'

'A special selection of antipasti,' intoned the waiter. 'Some very fine mozzarella – from the boss's uncle's herd of buffalo. In perfect condition. Some special Parma ham from a small village between Parma and Reggio-Emilia. Only available in five restaurants in the whole of Italy. Exclusive.'

'Very good,' said the cardinal. 'There's nothing wrong with exclusivity . . .' adding, quickly, 'as long as you are prepared to share it with others in a truly Christian spirit.'

The waiter nodded his agreement. 'Then we have a very nice tagliatelle,' he continued, 'with a porcini mushroom sauce and Sardinian artichokes.'

'Sardinian!' exclaimed the cardinal. 'That sounds very interesting.' He glanced at Pierre. 'Have you ever been to Sardinia, Monsieur Citroën?'

Pierre shook his head.

'Brigands,' whispered the cardinal.

The waiter suppressed a smile.

'Enrico here,' said the cardinal, 'is Sardinian . . . but not a brigand. Is that correct, Enrico?'

'Your Eminence is, as always, correct,' said the waiter.

'But not infallible,' said the cardinal. 'That epithet belongs to another altogether.'

The waiter smirked. 'Then there is ratatouille,' he said. 'A very subtle ratatouille.'

The cardinal made a gesture intended to say *Well, there you have it*. He turned to Pierre. 'I knew a Monsignor Ratatouille once, believe it or not. He was a senior figure in the Palace of the Holy Office. A charming man. A very considerable philatelist, as I recall. And of course you may have heard of dear Cardinal Casaroli, who became Vatican Secretary of State. He was a most skilful diplomat.'

'He was referred to in our course on international affairs,' said Pierre. 'I took an option on Eastern Europe and the Church. We were told he was highly instrumental in weakening the hold of the Soviet Union over countries behind the Iron Curtain.'

The cardinal agreed. 'They didn't like him one little bit,' he said, smiling at the memory. 'He was a real target for KGB spies, and they hate to be outwitted. They were desperate to know what he was up to.' He paused. 'In fact, poor Casaroli was spied upon for rather a long time. It's an extraordinary tale. Have you heard it?'

Pierre shook his head.

'It's a delicious story,' the cardinal went on. 'Casaroli was presented with a very fine ceramic statuette of the Virgin Mary – a present from a Czech lady of his acquaintance. He was very pleased to receive the gift, but unfortunately the statue had a small transmitter concealed in it. It was, as you say, bugged.'

Pierre's eyes widened. 'What a terrible thing to do,' he said.

The cardinal seemed pleased that Pierre had reacted in this way. 'I wholeheartedly agree,' he said. 'The gathering of intelligence is important, but there are limits to the means one employs. No cause is dignified by underhand methods.'

'Of course not.'

'And yet,' the cardinal went on, 'you cannot make an omelette without breaking at least some eggs.'

'Yes, that's true.'

The cardinal was now staring up at the ceiling. 'And fire, I believe, has to be fought with fire.'

'That's also true, Eminence.'

The cardinal lowered his gaze from the ceiling. 'The world is a difficult place, isn't it? Most of us would like not to get our hands dirty, but if we don't engage with the world, then we can hardly be surprised if the battalions of the wicked gain the upper hand.'

Pierre waited. He was unsure where this conversation was going, but the cardinal was an easy conversationalist and there was nothing strained about the exchange.

'Some people like to pretend that evil doesn't exist,' the cardinal went on. 'I believe that they are fundamentally mistaken. Evil is there, right under our noses sometimes, and it is tangible – and powerful. No amount of wishful thinking can will it out of existence. It is a fact. Evil is a brute fact and it can be seen in action every single day.'

'I'm sure you're right,' said Pierre.

The cardinal lowered his voice. 'So, the question with which we are confronted is this: how should we respond? Should we simply try to defeat evil through example – hoping that our good deeds will shame the perpetrators of evil? That's what the pacifists profess, isn't it? They say that if we simply opt out of the circle of violence and wrongdoing, then the repetitive cycle of such things will be broken. I can appreciate that argument. I understand what they're getting at. But . . .' He broke off. He looked downcast. 'But I find myself asking this question: what should we have done when confronted with the extermination camps of the Nazis? Should we have restricted ourselves to words, or should we have used force to liberate the remaining poor victims of that unimaginable cruelty and wickedness?'

He looked at Pierre, as if waiting for an answer. And that answer came quickly, as Pierre had no difficulty with this. 'We use all necessary force,' he said. 'We march up and dispose of the guards unless they surrender immediately, of course. We do anything and everything to stop any further acts of murder.'

The cardinal seemed surprised by the strength and speed of Pierre's response. 'I see that you have no reservations about that.'

'No, I don't.'

The cardinal nodded. 'I'm glad to hear that. So many, these days, are unprepared to defend the right. Their instinct is to appease, I'm afraid.' He paused. 'That, of course, is an historical example but there are many instances today, in our own times, where evil probes at our defences and where a robust response might be necessary.'

A further thought occurred to the cardinal. 'And of course, so many people today are relativists – which means that they seriously think it's impossible to distinguish between values. They take the view there's no such thing as truth – even scientific truth.'

'I know,' said Pierre. 'You hear those opinions all the time.'

'But they don't challenge Bernoulli's principle at thirty-six thousand feet,' observed the cardinal. He smiled, and continued, 'And what, I wonder, would these moral relativists say to some wretched victim of contemporary slavery or trafficking? Would they say there's no distinction to be made between your position and the position of the trafficker?'

'I don't think they would,' Pierre ventured.

'Then their relativism is inconsistent,' said the cardinal. 'They have to acknowledge that evil exists and that its condemnation requires the espousal of certain core values – human dignity, freedom, love of others, and so on.'

The waiter returned with the antipasti trolley, and began to help them to a selection.

'So delicious,' said the cardinal, spreading the starched

linen napkin out across his lap. 'Please begin, Pierre – if I may use your Christian name.'

'Of course, Your Em—'

The cardinal held up a hand. 'Please, don't bother about all that. I'm usually known as C. You may call me that, if you wish. It's a sort of . . . a sort of nickname, one might say.'

'Does it stand for anything?' asked Pierre.

'It's an abbreviation. I did once know what it stood for, but I never bother to explain to people. People think it's an initialism for Cardinal. That's a possibility, of course. But the point is, everybody calls me C.'

They embarked on the antipasti. After a mouthful of Parma ham, and one of delicate, almost liquid mozzarella, the cardinal dabbed at his lips with his pristine white napkin.

'Now then, Pierre,' he began, 'your dissertation on the *filioque* matter. I never imagined, when I delivered that lecture at the Gregorian, that I would have in my audience one who appreciated the finer points of that immensely complex issue. And then, at question time, in that dread silence when nobody seems to be willing to ask the first question – or even the second, for that matter – you came up with your very astute question. That certainly deserved a lunch, I thought.'

Pierre lowered his eyes modestly. The *filioque* was a minefield – it always had been – and he hoped that the cardinal would not expose the limits of his knowledge of the controversy too quickly. He had become interested in the whole question more or less by accident, having come across references to it in an article he read during his first month of study at the Gregorian. The title of the article had caught his attention for its sensationalist ring: *The phrase that tore the Church asunder – still dynamite today.* He had been intrigued; theological writing was seldom vivid, but this article presented the argument in a way that made the whole story of the schism between the Western and Eastern churches seem as if it was all happening no earlier than yesterday. He quickly became familiar with the kernel of the matter: the *filioque* clause, which meant *and from or by the son,* had been inserted into the Nicene creed by the Western Church. It referred to the origin of the Holy Spirit – or the Holy Ghost, as it was called by some. Where did the Holy Spirit come from? From the Father (God), from whom everything, after all, must come, or did the Son (Christ) have a role in creating it? The Church divided, with the Western Church adding a role for the Son, expressed in the term *filioque,* while the Eastern Church stuck to what it claimed was the original creed. In Orthodoxy, then, the Holy Spirit came from the Father and that was it. And the Western Church, Orthodoxy argued, had no right to add anything to the creed in this unilateral manner. The result was a schism in Christianity – not a small matter.

Pierre read more about the subject, and was amazed at how much there was. Rivers of ink had been spilled on the subject over the years, and passions were intense. He chose it as the subject of his dissertation, but even then he realised that he had hardly scratched the surface of the subject. And here was the cardinal, who had completed a doctorate on the *filioque*: how long would it take for him to realise, Pierre asked himself, that I know very little about the dispute? Of course, Rome was full of people with doctorates in the most obscure theological and ecclesiastical areas. The previous month he had met somebody with a doctorate in angelology, awarded, he learned, for a thesis on the subject of the various orders of angels and the gradations in their authority. Many PhDs, though, were based on very little, and some, he supposed, were concerned with the minutiae of things that did not exist at all. If he were ever to undertake doctoral studies, he suspected he would add to that vast body of writing that would never be read by anybody other than the examiners. But if so much scholarship was a glass-bead game, then it was a game that kept at least some people happy and harmed nobody. Angelology had never made anybody cry, had never sent anyone to bed hungry, had never come between friends ... He stopped himself: one had to be careful about making any such proposition about anything that might become an ideology. Millions had died for ideologies of one sort or another; countless people had been put to death because they could not give the right answer to some doctrinal question, or because they had been born in the wrong bed, to the wrong parents, or because they had forgotten the shibboleths that might have saved their lives. If there was one thing that humanity had always been good at, it was finding a reason to distrust or dislike others. The seed of that characteristic was there at the very beginning, implanted deep in our nature, only awaiting the slightest encouragement to flourish. *Them* and *us* began in children's games, and stayed with us until our last breath. Except, he thought; except when we cultivated a love of our fellow man, and that took such effort. Loving humanity in general, without distinction – in other words, acting as if all men were one's brothers – was, he thought, as difficult as being on a strict diet; it required much the same determination, much the same willpower. He wanted to do it; the urge to do so was there, and it was what had prompted him to the study of theology and philosophy in the first place, but he was not sure that he had within him the necessary strength, the necessary will. Alain was different: he sensed in him that current of love that the moral imperative required. That was why he could become a priest; that was why he could give up everything that the world had to offer in order to follow the example of the religious leader who, all those years ago, had spoken about love of others; a religious leader who made claims to divinity that he, Pierre, would love to believe but just could not. Not that his disbelief mattered, he thought; you could pretend to believe in things that you knew were unlikely to be true but that you knew offered hope in a damaged and unhappy world. We had to pretend – all the time we had to act as if certain things were true because we knew that otherwise our lives would be even more blighted than they currently were. It was like believing in Santa Claus when you were young; it was just like that. It was like whistling in the dark to keep your spirits up.

The cardinal made a number of comments on the question Pierre had asked at the lecture. 'I agree with you,' he said, 'that the Bonn Conference in 1874 came as close as we could expect at the time to bringing about a rapprochement between ourselves and our dear, misguided Orthodox brethren. Johann von Döllinger was really on to something when he said that the real issue is the precise meaning of the Latin verb *procedere*. You were right, I think, in saying that the problem was that the Greeks had two verbs doing similar work.

'So,' he continued, 'when the Latin creed says *who proceeded from the Father and the Son (Filioque)*, it does not mean that the Holy Spirit came *equally* from both. It is perfectly possible, within the meaning of the Latin verb, that the Holy Spirit originated in the Father ...'

'It must have,' said Pierre, 'because the Father is the source of all creation. Everything comes from God – it must do, as long as one believes that there is a god.'

'Precisely,' said the cardinal. 'But something that is passed *through* another being can surely be said to *proceed* through that being. That's the point that von Döllinger wanted to stress. And I think it provided us with a real opportunity to put division behind us.'

185

'But it was premature?'

'I think so. I know that the issue had been discussed for a very long time – ever since the days of Origen and Gregory Thaumaturgus in the third century. I know that it was the subject of intense debate between East and West. I know there has been a lot of hurt involved, but these things take time. There is a chance, though, that we might be getting to the point where a compromise might be possible.'

'But we would have to drop the *filioque* from the creed? Would the Orthodox brethren accept anything less than that?'

The cardinal sighed. 'Some would. Others ... well, you know what human nature is like. It has become a matter of pride for some. And there's an additional point. There's the issue of whether they acknowledge that we had the right to insert clauses into the creed. They're sticky about that. They don't accept our authority to change the creed in that way.'

Pierre agreed that this was a serious stumbling block. 'Will the Orthodox churches ever accept the primacy of His Holiness?'

'Once again, there are shades of opinion,' said the cardinal. 'But no, I don't think they will. They would be prepared to work with us on the basis of equality, I imagine, but what would that entail? I imagine that it would require that any change in the creed be agreed by both ourselves and Orthodoxy. And the point is: we are not equal. We have apostolic succession and will not give that up.'

For a short while Pierre said nothing. He felt the eyes of the cardinal upon him, as if his reaction to what was being said was being carefully weighed. He took a sip of his glass of mineral water. Then he said, 'It's a great pity, because I'm not sure that it matters terribly much whether the Son had a role in the creation of the Holy Spirit. What matters is the Holy Spirit is there, working in the world to help men to see what might be.' As he said this, he thought, *How can anyone seriously believe that the Holy Spirit is a person? Yet that is what I seem to be saying.*

The cardinal frowned. 'I understand why you should feel that way,' he said. 'But we need to be certain, don't we? We need to be certain as to where the Holy Spirit fits in. The Greeks would say that we are effectively demoting the Holy Spirit to a subsidiary place – the junior position within the Trinity. I don't agree, of course; I feel that there is nothing undignified about proceeding from the Son, who is, after all, *of one nature with the Father.* That's crucial, in my view – absolutely crucial.'

They discussed the *filioque* issue for a further twenty minutes or so, until it was time for dessert, a cassata of which the cardinal had two helpings. Then it was time for coffee, by which point they had left the *filioque* and moved on to a discussion of a special exhibition about to open at the Vatican Museum. This was a display of artefacts and documents connected with Jesuit missions in Goa. And that was the subject in which they were still immersed when the cardinal suddenly looked out of the window and saw his car draw up outside the restaurant.

'My driver,' he explained to Pierre. 'I'm afraid that I'm going to have to dash. I've enjoyed our conversation immensely, Pierre, and I wish you all luck with your future. Perhaps a doctorate on the *filioque* – or something similar. The world is so full of possibilities, isn't it?'

Pierre watched as the cardinal was ushered out of the restaurant by Enrico. Directly outside the restaurant a sleek green car had drawn up, and a driver, clad in simple ministerial garb, was stepping out. He opened the car door for the cardinal, who nodded to him as he stepped inside.

The car was an Aston Martin.

Pierre sat down. He was uncertain what to think. The lunch had been a success, he thought, as the cardinal had gone away in good humour after they finished their wide-ranging discussion. Before he left, though, he had said, 'My secretary might be in touch. We'll see.'

Who was this *we*? Pierre wondered. And what were they expecting to see? Why, indeed, were they bothering to look in the first place? Pierre was asking himself these questions as he prepared to leave the restaurant a few minutes after the cardinal had made his departure. He was shown out by Enrico, all courtesy and solicitude, who, as he opened the front door for him, slipped a piece of paper into his hand.

'Read that later,' he whispered.

Pierre waited until he had gone round the corner before

he unfolded the note. It had obviously been hurriedly written, but the words were clear enough. *Be careful*, it said. That was all.

He heard nothing from the cardinal's office for the next two weeks, and had begun to think that the entire episode was at an end. It was a strange thing to have happened, but in his experience, there were plenty of stranger things that happened in Rome. He wrote to his parents to tell them that he had been invited to lunch by a cardinal, and his mother wrote back to say that she had once met a cardinal who was a distant relative of her godmother. She could not remember his name, she said, nor could she recall anything that he said, but she did remember his scarlet biretta. 'I hope you made a good impression,' she said. 'These chances do not come up very often in this life.'

No, he thought, they do not, and he was unlikely to receive another invitation like that. But then, one morning he received a further telephone call from Father Heaney.

'Monsieur Citroën,' began the priest, 'I know that this is no notice at all, but if you happen to be free this morning, I wonder if we could possibly meet. I won't take up much of your time – an hour or so would be more than enough. There's a matter I should like to discuss with you.'

Pierre accepted the invitation. He did so automatically – as he was free that morning – but, even as he did so, he recalled the scribbled note passed to him by the waiter at

La Regola. But it was too late now to remember a prior engagement.

'Good,' said Father Heaney. 'I suggest we meet in the Borghese Gardens. Perhaps in front of the Galleria Borghese itself. Are you familiar with the gallery?'

'I have been there,' said Pierre. It occurred to him, though, that not having met Father Heaney before he was not sure that he would recognise him. Of course, if he were in clerical dress, it would be easy enough – unless, of course, the Borghese Gardens happened to be teeming with priests at the time – which was always possible in Rome.

'Father, I must ask: how will I know you?' he asked. 'We've never actually met, have we?'

The priest did not reply immediately, but then he said, 'Don't worry, I shall recognise you.'

Pierre wanted to ask how, but before he could say anything, Father Heaney explained, 'We have a photograph, you see.' This made Pierre catch his breath, but before anything else could be said the priest brought the conversation to an end. Now, Pierre sat at his desk, gazing out of his window at the sun-drenched sky of Rome. He should have asked the priest what it was he wanted to discuss. In fact, he felt it would have been more courteous for Father Heaney to give him some indication of the discussion he had in mind, rather than to assume, rather imperiously, that the invitation would be accepted without question. But then he reminded himself: this was a cardinal's office with which he was dealing, and presumably a cardinal's office could do very much as it wanted when engaging with a lowly student.

He looked at his watch. His meeting with Father Heaney was to be at eleven thirty, and it was now barely nine. It would not take him more than three-quarters of an hour to get to the Villa Borghese by foot, and yet, feeling distracted and slightly on edge, he did not relish the thought of sitting in his room until it was time to set off. He made up his mind: he would take his time walking to the Borghese Gardens and once there he could sit on a bench and watch the world pass by until it was time to meet Father Heaney.

Like all city parks, the vast sprawl of the Borghese Gardens performed a multitude of roles: the elegant landscape was a haven for refugees from the busy streets of the city; a retreat for lovers in search of privacy; an inspiration for visitors seeking a vision of classical order. But it was also, to the practised and suspicious eye, a haven for clandestine encounters ranging from the relatively innocent to the unambiguously sinister. Like any public space in Italy, of course, it was a place for display – for the parade of *la bella figura* – even by dogs, brought here by their owners to the special area known as the Valley of the Dogs, where Roman canines strolled and strutted with a sense of style quite lacking in the dogs of lesser cities.

After a few minutes of walking aimlessly along one of the peripheral paths Pierre found himself looking out over the lake to the Temple of Asclepius. The water was still, and the temple was reflected in its surface, the building's pillars casting tall white lines across the green surface of the lake. He found a bench under an ancient pine tree, and sat down in the shade the tree provided. Although the morning had not yet reached its hottest point, the air was already heavy and sluggish, needing rain to wash it clean. There was silence, but it was that attenuated silence of a great city, the site of a million conversations, the backdrop to the movement, backwards and forwards, of hundreds of thousands of people earning their living. And there was a bird somewhere, too; a bird singing a pure note against the inescapable hum of the city. Pierre closed his eyes, and thought about what Father Heaney might say to him, and what his response should be. Was he being sucked into something – one of those murky intrigues for which the Vatican was famous, and about which Enrico, the waiter, had so bluntly warned him? Was he being picked up? For all he knew, the cardinal had regular meetings with young men approached on his behalf by his secretary. The Church was no stranger to such matters, which was its own fault, Pierre thought: anybody with the slightest knowledge of human psychology knew that a culture of denial and repression would never subdue the demands of the libido: how could it? Or was he simply being helped in some yet to be identified way by a powerful man who had discovered that an obscure student shared an intellectual interest – the *filioque* controversy – and had wanted to do something to mark his pleasure in this discovery?

Influential, successful people took pleasure in helping those at the beginning of their careers – there was nothing sinister in that and no objective grounds for imagining that the cardinal and his secretary might be harbouring some ulterior objective. He took a deep breath: he would put suspicion in its place, keep an open mind and, for the moment at least, assume good faith on the part of the Benedictine and his exalted employer.

It was while he was sitting beside the lake that Pierre became aware of two figures further along the shore. Two men were standing at the water's edge, engaged in conversation while they gazed across the lake at the temple on the other side. Pierre was sufficiently far away from them, and shaded enough by the pine tree, not to be noticed by them, but close enough to catch the occasional word of their exchange.

Discreetly, he threw a glance in their direction, noticing that one of them was tall and bearded, while the other, sleeker and shorter, was dressed in clerical garb and was wearing a black biretta. There was no incongruity in this, of course, even if others in the gardens were less formally dressed: this was Rome, after all, a city in which clerical figures were not at all out of place. But Pierre's conclusion was immediate: the man in the biretta was Father James Heaney, OSB. He could be no other. And what brought him to that conclusion was his overhearing of a single expression, dropped into the morning air of the Borghese Gardens as if by parachute: *filioque*. The two men at the water's edge, believing themselves unobserved, were discussing the *filioque* controversy.

Before he slipped away, sidling off his bench so as not to be noticed, Pierre heard one or two other snippets of the conversation. He heard the word 'Nicene' and then 'patriarch', and then a couple of unmistakably Greek names, 'Angelos Evangelis' and then 'Aristomenis Petronannos', neither of which he recognised, but which conveyed the flavour of the discussion. And then, again, the expression *filioque*, clearly enunciated, removing all doubt about what was going on. Or creating exactly that doubt?

Neither of the men seemed to notice Pierre and after following a path for a few minutes, he felt himself safe enough to turn back and look in their direction. They were still there, still apparently deep in conversation, although the priest was now reaching into a pocket and extracting something – an envelope, Pierre thought – which the other man examined briefly, nodded, and then slipped into a thin briefcase he was carrying.

Pierre hesitated; if the conversation was coming to an end, he did not want Father Heaney suddenly to see him staring in his direction. And it was now almost eleven fifteen, and he would need to make his way towards the gallery, outside which he and the secretary were shortly due to meet. As he walked in that direction, he thought of what he had seen. Looked at from one angle, it was nothing special. Father

Heaney – and he was convinced that one of the men was him – had simply bumped into a friend in the gardens while on his way to his arranged meeting outside the gallery. There was nothing odd in that: even in a city as big as Rome one might have a chance encounter with one whom one knew. And if that friend whom one happened to meet was a theologian, or an ecclesiastical historian – of whom there would be so many in a place like Rome – then what could be more natural and unsurprising than that one might have a conversation about the *filioque* and some of the figures involved in the debate? But looked at in a different way, there were features of the situation that might make one stop and think. Firstly, there was the appearance of the taller figure. He was thin-faced and bearded, and he had about him, even when seen from a distance, that characteristic bony appearance of an Orthodox priest. There was no essential reason why Orthodox priests should look the way they did, but that was how it was, at least to Pierre. And the beard, of course, spoke volumes.

Suddenly he stopped. It could not have been a chance encounter that he witnessed. An envelope had been exchanged, an envelope containing money or documents, and one did not exchange an envelope with a friend whom one just happened to meet while out for a walk. No, there was something going on, and Pierre thought that whatever it was had not been intended for other eyes.

He turned a corner and saw the impressive shape of the

gallery appear behind the trees. He was now beginning to feel anxious and for a moment or two he considered turning on his heels and leaving. He could contact Father Heaney and give him some excuse for missing their meeting, and if the priest suggested another time or place he could find some reason for being unable to make it. That should bring an end to the matter, as they – Father Heaney and the cardinal – would be subtle enough to realise that Pierre was discouraging any further approach.

He had almost decided to do that when he heard a voice behind him. It seemed to come from behind a yew hedge, but in fact it was from a path that joined the path on which Pierre had been walking. And there, when Pierre turned round, was the man he had seen beside the lake.

'There you are!' said Father Heaney, extending a hand. 'I do hope I'm not late.'

They shook hands. Pierre noticed that the priest's palm was warm to the touch – as if he had exerted himself in a brisk walk.

'Such a fine day,' Father Heaney continued. 'Mind you, just about every day in Rome is fine at this time of year. Not too hot – although it's heating up a bit – but certainly nothing like August. Oh, my goodness, August can be a trial, but I suppose you've always been up in France in August – a much more bearable place at that time of year.'

'Yes,' said Pierre, giving Father Heaney a shy glance. The priest's expression was an open one, his manner warm and friendly. There was nothing threatening about him, and Pierre found himself regretting his earlier suspicions.

They began to walk towards the gallery. 'I thought we might take a look at some of the paintings,' said Father Heaney. 'I never tire of visiting this gallery. It doesn't matter how many times you see a favourite painting – there's always something new to be noticed.' He paused. 'Do you have a favourite artist?'

Pierre shrugged. 'My tastes are fairly broad. I like the obvious ones. Titian, I suppose. Botticelli, of course. I love the *Primavera*, for instance.'

Father Heaney turned to him enthusiastically. 'Now there's a case in point. I said that we always seem able to notice fresh things about a familiar painting. *Primavera* has more meaning packed into its details than one might imagine. Into every bit of it. The subjects in Botticelli's paintings *gaze* a great deal, and that particular painting is no exception. Hermes-Mercurius, for instance, is portrayed looking up at a concealed god, somewhere behind the hanging fruit in the painting. He sees what we cannot see, *and yet we know it's there.*'

He paused, and looked at Pierre as if waiting for some sign of agreement.

'I see,' said Pierre. 'I mean: I see what you mean – I'm not claiming to see what isn't there.'

Father Heaney laughed. 'I understand,' he said. 'There's a book you might care to read. It's called *Under the Guise of*

Spring, and it's all about the hidden messages in that painting. Just *Primavera* – just that painting.' He hesitated before
continuing. He cleared his throat. 'Of course, not everything
is what it seems, is it? The world may seem intelligible enough
to us – we may think we understand it – but the real meaning
of the phenomena we observe may be quite different from
what we think it is.'

'I suppose that's right,' said Pierre. 'And yet we can't go
through life assuming that there's a hidden meaning to
everything. We'd all end up like those conspiracy theorists
who argue that black, whenever we encounter it, is really
white, and vice versa.'

Father Heaney appeared to weigh this. 'That's true,' he
said at last. 'And yet what if there really are conspiracies – as
there must be? At least some. If we are excessively sceptical
then wouldn't we discount them all – even the ones that
actually exist?'

Pierre agreed. 'I'm not suggesting we take everything at
face value,' he said. 'All that I'm saying is that as a general
rule, what we see is what there is.'

'That depends on how general your rule is,' Father Heaney
responded. 'But look, let's go in and look out the Caravaggio.
I take it you like Caravaggio. Of course you do. Who could
not like Caravaggio?'

Pierre nodded. He had his reservations, though.
Caravaggio in his mind was all about rough trade and violence, really, a world of taverns and knife-fights, and the

darkness that always lay behind the light. Botticelli was more to his taste, he felt, with his flowers and seashells and women clad in diaphanous garments. He was altogether lighter, no matter what hidden meanings art historians might read into his every brush stroke.

They strolled through the gallery, that at that hour of the morning was largely empty of other visitors. Father Heaney proved to be a well-informed guide, drawing Pierre's attention to the works of artists whom Pierre had not encountered before, and seeming to know an impressive amount about them. It was to Caravaggio, though, that he seemed most drawn.

Standing before *Boy with a Basket of Fruit*, Father Heaney shook his head in sheer admiration. 'Look at the detail on the fruit,' he said. 'What a delectable offering. Look at the peach – one might reach forward and eat it, don't you think?'

'Possibly,' said Pierre.

'And there's another thing,' continued Father Heaney. 'Some of the fruit is diseased. Caravaggio is so determined to convey the truth of what he sees that he has put traces of blight on one of the apples and there, you'll see, is a vine leaf with fungal spots.'

Pierre peered.

'And as for the boy himself,' Father Heaney said, 'he was one Mario Minniti, who appears in a number of Caravaggio's works. He was a Sicilian and was involved with Caravaggio in the street fight that led to the death of Ranuccio Tommasoni.

He was a somewhat unsavoury young man, I suppose, but we all have our little faults – in some cases, not so little, perhaps.'

Pierre smiled. 'Let he who is without sin cast the first stone,' he said.

'Precisely,' said Father Heaney. He hesitated, as if uncertain whether to say something, but then he remarked, 'Do you believe in the existence of good and evil, Pierre? I mean, not just vague concepts of good and evil, but actual good and evil that you can see and touch?'

Pierre looked away. He did not like probing questions like this. He did not like being asked whether he believed in God, even though he studied theology and was in attendance at a pontifical university. He considered these issues private, although he accepted that in many respects they were very public matters on which a stand might need to be taken. *Perhaps I lack courage*, he thought.

'I think I do,' he said.

'Just think?'

'Yes. It's just that I'm not sure whether the dividing lines are always as clear as all that.'

Pierre was aware that the Benedictine was staring at him through narrowed eyes. For a few moments he thought that he had overstepped the mark – that Father Heaney would take offence at his condescending answer – not that he had intended to condescend, but that was the way it must have sounded. But the cleric relaxed, and then bowed his head in a gesture of assent. 'You're right. You're quite right. These things are complex ... And yet, even if they are nuanced, right and wrong still exist, as I'm sure you will agree.'

Pierre seized the opportunity to make amends. 'Of course. Yes, I completely agree.'

Father Heaney came closer to him. They were alone in one of the rooms of the gallery; alone with Caravaggio and Ghirlandaio, and a few other silent witnesses. He lowered his voice. 'Monsieur Citroën, I have been asked by His Eminence to ...' His voice lowered even further. Now it was not much more than a whisper. '... to sound you out about an offer of employment. I believe that you have no firm plans as yet as to what to do after graduation.'

Pierre found himself whispering his response. 'No, I don't.'

'Good. Well, as you may or may not know, we have our own secret service.'

Pierre gave an involuntary start.

'No, you should not be surprised. The Holy See is a state. We have international legal personality. We have diplomatic representation and we accredit ambassadors here at the Vatican. We have a police force and the Swiss Guards, who are a militia. We have a railway station and courts and we make treaties. We have observer status at the United Nations. In view of all that, it makes sense that we should have a secret service as well.'

For a few moments, Pierre said nothing. Then he whispered, 'I understand.'

'Our secret service used to be called the Holy Alliance,'

Father Heaney continued. 'Today it is called the Entity. It is one of the oldest, if not *the* oldest secret service in the world. Five centuries is a long history in espionage.

'We are staffed by a mixture of lay and clerical agents. I believe in calling a spade a spade, and so I don't mind using the term *spy*. We have spies in all the world's major capitals. We share intelligence with sympathetic agencies. We have worked with Mossad and with MI6. We have pitted our wits against the opposition in the form of the NKVD and KGB, as it was in its earlier incarnations. We know a great deal, Monsieur Citroën, about everything. We are shocked by nothing. *Nihil humanum mihi alienum est*, I always say.

'Of course, we need to recruit, and that is something that we do with great caution. Every agent is vetted personally by C, as His Eminence is known in the service. If he disapproves of a potential recruit, then the matter stops right there. If he approves, then the candidate embarks on a one-year training programme. This includes cryptology, the trade craft of espionage, electronic monitoring techniques, and theology. In your case, you would be exempted from the theological element because you have already studied theology to degree level.

'It is not a career without danger. We have lost good agents in our battle against the forces of evil. There are pitfalls at every turn. The hours are long. It is difficult, sometimes, for our lay agents to have a normal family life, as they may have to travel a great deal. However, we do what we can to ensure that the needs of our staff are met. We have a very good dental care programme.

'Engagement is for a period of five years initially, although people may leave at any time if their conscience dictates it or if they lose their faith in what we are doing. Everybody within the service believes in the rectitude of our mission. We could not operate were it not for that complete dedication.'

Father Heaney stopped. 'I have given you rather a lot to think about, I suspect. You will no doubt wish to consider what I have said before you give us your answer. His Eminence, though, would appreciate a decision by next Tuesday, if possible.' He reached into his pocket and took out a slip of paper, which he passed on to Pierre. 'Here is his direct line. I shall drop out of the process after this, as he prefers to deal directly with recruits. You will not hear from me again.'

The cleric looked at him, his expression serious at first. Then his face broke into a smile. 'I imagine you didn't anticipate this when you agreed to meet me today.'

Pierre returned the smile. There was a release of tension now, on both sides. 'No, I wasn't sure what to expect. I had thought I might be offered a scholarship or something of that sort – but not a job. And certainly not a job of this nature.'

'Nobody ever does,' said Father Heaney. 'It is my lot in life to surprise people.'

They began to make their way out of the gallery. It was warm outside, now – almost too warm to stand in the sun.

They stood there and prepared to say goodbye, as they were going off in different directions. Pierre suddenly said, 'I saw you earlier on, I think.'

Father Heaney looked up. 'Me?'

'Yes. I saw you by the lake. I guessed it was you – and I was right.'

Somewhere behind them in the gardens a cicada struck up its shrill call.

'You were talking to a friend,' Pierre continued.

Father Heaney did not respond. Pierre felt uncomfortable. The congenial atmosphere of their earlier meeting had now been replaced by something very different. *Perhaps I should not have said that*, thought Pierre.

'I think you were mistaken,' said Father Heaney. 'There are many people in the gardens. You must have seen somebody else.'

Pierre was taken aback by the abrupt denial. Did the secretary seriously expect him to deny the evidence of his own senses? He felt annoyed. He would not be doubted in this way.

'I couldn't help but overhear you,' he said. 'I think you were discussing the *filioque* issue.' That, he thought, would show Father Heaney that he was not imagining things.

The secretary's eyes narrowed. 'I think you are compounding your mistake, Monsieur Citroën,' he said. 'And if I were you, I would say no more about it.' He paused. 'I take it that you understand me?'

Pierre swallowed. There was a note of icy menace in the other man's voice, and all he wanted now was to be away from him. Enrico was right, he thought. These people are not to be engaged with lightly. 'I'm sorry,' he said. 'Subject closed.'

'Good,' said Father Heaney, abruptly, and turned on his heel. He did not say goodbye.

The following Monday, Pierre spoke to his ecclesiastical history professor, an American Jesuit, Monsignor Henry Downside. The monsignor was a helpful man whom he had always found approachable, and who seemed to know everything there was to know about the complex history of the Church. He had written a commentary on the history of the papacy, a multi-volume work that ran to over four thousand closely printed pages. And even that generous allocation had obliged him, he confessed, to omit a great deal of detail that he would, in an ideal world, have wished to include.

'Professor,' Pierre began, 'do you know much about the Vatican secret service?'

The monsignor smiled. 'I hope I don't know too much,' he said, looking over his shoulder in a theatrical way. 'There are some topics about which it is wise not to have too much knowledge – if you get my meaning.'

Pierre considered this. Once again, he realised that he was being warned – although the warning on this occasion was a veiled one.

'Having said that,' the monsignor continued, 'there is a

great deal of information about these people that is there in the history books – and much of it is distasteful. Certainly, if one looks at the activities of the Holy Alliance in the past, one is struck by its utter ruthlessness. The seventeenth century, for example, was particularly unedifying. That, as you may recall from my lectures – if you were indeed listening, dear Monsieur Citroën . . .' And here the monsignor smiled in that gentle, accepting way of professors who know that not all their students remain awake throughout their lectures . . . 'as I am sure you were, of course, then you will recall that at that point the Vatican was a hotbed of intrigue and deeply involved in power struggles within France and Spain.'

The monsignor sighed as he contemplated the labyrinthine complexities of European courts of the age. 'However, temporal power, I suppose, inevitably involves a struggle for dominance. And that means that agents of the powerful will be pitted against one another, spying on each other, doing whatever they can to advance their particular cause. Such is human nature.'

That observation prompted a further sigh. 'I might give you an example,' he went on. 'Espionage provokes counter-espionage. During the reign of Louis XIV, French spies were particularly active in Rome and they even succeeded in establishing a network within the Vatican's secretariat of state. They had three priests in the Vatican archives department. Their job was to copy documents – which they did. They made extra copies, though, and passed these on to France's representatives in Rome. The Vatican suspected this was going on, having learned that there was a network of spies and that its leader had the code-name of Scipio. That has a modern ring to it, doesn't it? Major spies in our own times have often had classical-sounding code-names. Nothing changes, you see, Monsieur Citroën: very little in human affairs is new. But then, I am an historian, and I suppose people would expect me to say that.'

The professor continued his story. 'Let us return,' he said, 'to a fresh spring day in May, 1687 – only yesterday, in Church history terms. The head of the Vatican's spy network at the time was one Cardinal Paluzzi, a man of considerable power. He was told by his agents that the document-copying departments always seemed to make one more copy of every confidential document than was required. What happened to these extra copies? Minolta spy cameras did not exist in those days, of course, and a spy could hardly carry a portable camera obscura with him . . .'

Pierre realised that this was a joke, and he smiled, even if so belatedly that Monsignor Downside looked a bit disappointed.

'Anyway,' continued the cleric, 'Cardinal Paluzzi ordered his toughest agents, the monks of the Black Order, to arrest one of the copyists – a monk himself – and to torture him until he revealed the names of his fellow spies. He was then killed and hung up from beneath a bridge. Attached to the body was a small piece of black cloth with two red stripes on it. That was the calling card of the Black Order.'

He paused, and Pierre wondered whether this was to emphasise that he should remember this detail.

'Since then, the methods of the Holy Alliance have become less, how shall I put it, less robust? But they still operate in the murky world of espionage and consort with toughened agents of the secret services of other states. There is nothing you can teach the Holy See about survival, you know. They are not naïve. Nor are they unworldly. They know where their interest lies and they will pursue that with all the determination of those who are satisfied that right is on their side.'

The monsignor paused to draw breath. Suddenly his expression changed, as if a thought had just occurred to him. 'Have you been *approached*, Monsieur Citroën?' he asked.

Pierre hesitated. He had not intended to reveal any details of his conversation with Father Heaney, but it seemed that Monsignor Downside had guessed what had prompted his interest. He hesitated, but he was by nature frank and did not want to hide the truth from his professor. 'Yes,' he replied at last. 'They've spoken to me – indirectly, of course, but they made their intentions clear enough.'

The monsignor absorbed this information gravely. 'And have you responded?'

Pierre shook his head. 'I have to let them know by tomorrow.'

'They haven't given you much time.'

'No. And I find myself uncertain as to what to do. A bit of me is flattered by the invitation. Lots of people would love to be asked to be a spy, wouldn't they?'

The monsignor raised an eyebrow. 'It appeals to a certain sort, perhaps. Many spies are misfits. They may be people who have been disappointed by the world. They may be people wanting to settle old scores with a fate that has not given them what they feel they are entitled to in life. They may be locked in battle with a deceased parent or they may be looking for a father. They may think that espionage will give them an importance that they don't have in their ordinary life. They may want approval, and find it in the praise given them by their handler. There may be many factors at play, many of them based on some pathology of the soul.'

Pierre was silent. It was obvious to him that Professor Downside considered spying to be a very inferior occupation.

'Of course,' the monsignor went on, 'the decision must be yours. I would not presume to influence you in any way, but you should be aware of the nature of the choice you are being asked to make. Do you want to spend your life in the shadows? Now there *are* shadows, and it is the lot of some to work within them or, indeed, on their periphery, in their liminal territory. But if you are one who prefers to be in the clear light of day, then perhaps it is best not to dwell in penumbral regions. That's all I am saying – no more than that.' He paused. 'Do you get the drift of what I'm saying?'

Pierre nodded. 'I understand, Professor.'

'Good,' said Monsignor Downside. 'That is all that I could wish for in any of my students' understanding.'

That evening, Pierre knocked on the door of his friend, Alain, further down the corridor in the students' living quarters. He heard his friend's voice reply from within and he entered the room. Alain was at his desk, struggling with a passage of New Testament Greek. He looked up at his friend and smiled. 'You know something, Pierre? You're really fortunate you don't have to learn Greek. Never, ever forget that.'

'At least it isn't Finnish,' said Pierre. 'I gather that's a really difficult language.'

'That's why there are only five million Finns,' said Alain. 'If Finnish were easier, then there would be far more of them.'

Pierre laughed.

'By the way,' said Alain. 'Who was your monastic friend?'

Pierre looked puzzled. 'Friend?' he asked. 'I'm sorry, I don't know what you mean.'

'Your visitor, earlier today.'

Pierre shook his head. 'I didn't have a visitor.'

'Well, I saw him coming out of your room,' Alain explained. 'I was coming back to my room and I saw him coming out of your door. He didn't see me, but I saw him. He disappeared down the corridor.'

Pierre's puzzlement deepened. 'A monk?'

'Well, he was in monastic garb.'

'Did you see his face?' asked Pierre.

'No. I didn't.'

Pierre sat down. 'I need to tell you about something,' he said.

He started with the letter from the cardinal. Then he went on to describe seeing Father Heaney and his furtive meeting beside the lake. Finally, he recounted his conversation with Monsignor Downside. Alain listened without interrupting him. When he had finished, he rose from his seat and went to gaze out of the window. It was from there that he addressed his friend, not turning round as he spoke.

'There's only one conclusion you can draw about this Heaney character,' he said. 'He's a double agent. You saw him meeting with a contact from the other side. He must have been passing him sensitive documents. It's a classic drop, as they call it in espionage circles.'

Pierre wondered what the documents might have been.

'Something to do with the *filioque* controversy,' said Alain. 'You said you heard them talking about that.'

'But ...' began Pierre.

He was interrupted. 'You need to tell C. You have to warn him.'

Pierre was about to reply to this when he stopped himself. *How did Alain know about* C? He had said nothing about that being the cardinal's acronym. He was positive about that, which suggested that Alain knew more than he might be owning up to knowing.

211

He decided to test his supposition. 'You mean the cardinal?' he asked.

Alain replied quite naturally. 'Yes, him . . .' Then his voice trailed away as he realised that he had fallen into a trap.

Now Pierre was certain. 'How do you know about C?' he asked.

Alain opened his mouth to reply, then he closed it. He turned round to face his friend. 'Because I'm in the Entity,' he said quietly. 'I have been one of its agents for over a year now. I'm on a Holy Alliance scholarship here – all my fees are paid – and any dental costs.'

That was all the confirmation Pierre needed. He remembered that Father Heaney had said something about the secret service's dental plan. Alain knew about it, and that meant he was telling the truth.

'I don't know what to do,' he said weakly. 'What if Father Heaney finds out that I've reported him to C as a possible double agent?'

Alain looked sympathetic. 'You'll be in danger,' he said.

'I don't know what to do,' Pierre repeated, his voice cracking with emotion. 'I never asked to get caught up in all this *filioque* business.'

Alain understood. 'I agree, your position is rather sensitive.' He thought for a moment. Then he suggested that they go to Pierre's room and check to see if anything had been disturbed. 'They may have planted a bug,' said Alain. 'That's the sort of thing they do.'

They went quickly down the corridor and Pierre unlocked his door. Once in his room, Alain raised a finger to his lips to signify the need for silence. Pierre nodded his assent. Then he saw what had happened. He pointed to an open drawer in his desk. Tearing a piece of paper from a notebook he wrote: *My notes on the* filioque *controversy – gone.*

Alain read the note. He looked grave. Then he wrote his reply, *You should get out immediately – like now! Pronto!*

Monsignor Downside was both helpful and reassuring. When Pierre went to see him the following day, he listened carefully to what he had to say about the break-in and the removal of his notes on the *filioque* controversy. After he had finished, he shook his head sadly. 'Typical of their methods,' he said. 'Typical.'

'I want to go home,' said Pierre. 'I want to go home to France. I want to return to Bordeaux.'

'That sounds very wise,' said the monsignor. 'You know what my favourite Bordeaux wine is? I'll tell you: Pauillac. I have some 2009 in my cellar. Gorgeous. And I have two cases of 2015 Margaux – a secondary wine from a very good estate and therefore a terrific bargain.'

'Will you be able to speak to the college?' asked Pierre. 'I've almost finished my course. I could write my final exam in Bordeaux – under supervision, of course.'

'I shall make it my business to ensure that you get per-mission to do just that,' said Monsignor Downside. 'I also have some rather good Graves, you know. Last time I was in Bordeaux I visited several of the chateaux there. I also went to Sauternes and tried some dry Sauternes. People forget that they make dry Sauternes – and some of it is very fine indeed. Did you know that you can have Sauternes with *pâté de foie gras*? Did you know that? People think that you should only have it with dessert, but they are very wrong, you know.'

Pierre returned to Bordeaux two days later. His parents met him at the airport, where his mother flung her arms about him and his father, grinning with pleasure, slapped his shoulder several times. The following week he wrote his final examination under the supervision of the deputy principal of a local technical college. He achieved a distinction in that subject, as well as an overall distinction in his degree results.

'What now?' asked his father.

It was a question that Pierre knew he could answer in such a way as to make his father happy. That answer, though, also reflected what he now knew he wanted himself. 'I'd like to be a wine *négociant*, Father. Will you take me into the business?'

'Oh, my dear boy,' said his father, struggling to hold back his tears. 'My heart is overflowing with joy.'

Pierre proved to have all of his father's abilities – and even more. He made astute purchases of parcels of fine wines and found a good market for them. The customers liked him. Sometimes he discussed theology with them, but not very often, which was a relief to the customers.

Two years later he married Annette de Quarante-Cinq, the daughter of a couple who owned a small chateau and a moderately productive vineyard. Their wines were highly regarded and were even served by Air France – in economy class. Pierre was welcomed into the family, as his new father-in-law had blood pressure issues and was keen to retire. After his retirement, le Comte de Quarante-Cinq and his wife went to live in the Auvergne, where they had a house on top of a hill and where his blood pressure tended to come down. It was something to do with altitude, he explained, but Pierre was not sure whether there was any medical basis to the explanation.

Pierre and Annette ran the vineyard. They had two daughters, both of whom were keen dancers. Pierre never thought again of the *filioque* issue, although one evening he had a dream in which he was back in Rome, in the Borghese Gardens, he thought. He came across a man sitting on a bench who turned to him, and said, in the dream, 'You know something about the *filioque*? It doesn't matter. It just doesn't matter.'

And then he awoke, and he was back in their comfortable small chateau, in the early morning, with the shoots of a creeper tapping at the window, and the sun on the vines and distant hilltops, and the sound of the wind, the gentle wind, which might have been a spirit, perhaps, and possibly was. Who knew?

He got out of bed. It was a big day at the winery: wine

that had spent two years in the barrel was bottled. He was pleased with the vintage in question and had high hopes for it, as had several wine writers. They had been enthusiastic, and one of them, the correspondent of a major American wine magazine, was coming for lunch that day. Pierre would present him with a signed bottle in an oak case.

The wine writer arrived shortly before lunch. Pierre met him outside the chateau and showed him into the cellar. 'Here,' he said, reaching for the bottle they had prepared for their visitor. 'Here is our new wine.'

The writer looked at the label. '*Filioque?*' he asked. 'Nice name for a wine.'

'Do you think so?'

The writer nodded. 'Yes. Good choice.' He paused. He looked puzzled. 'What does it mean?'

Pierre smiled. 'It's complicated,' he said. 'And it's time for lunch.'